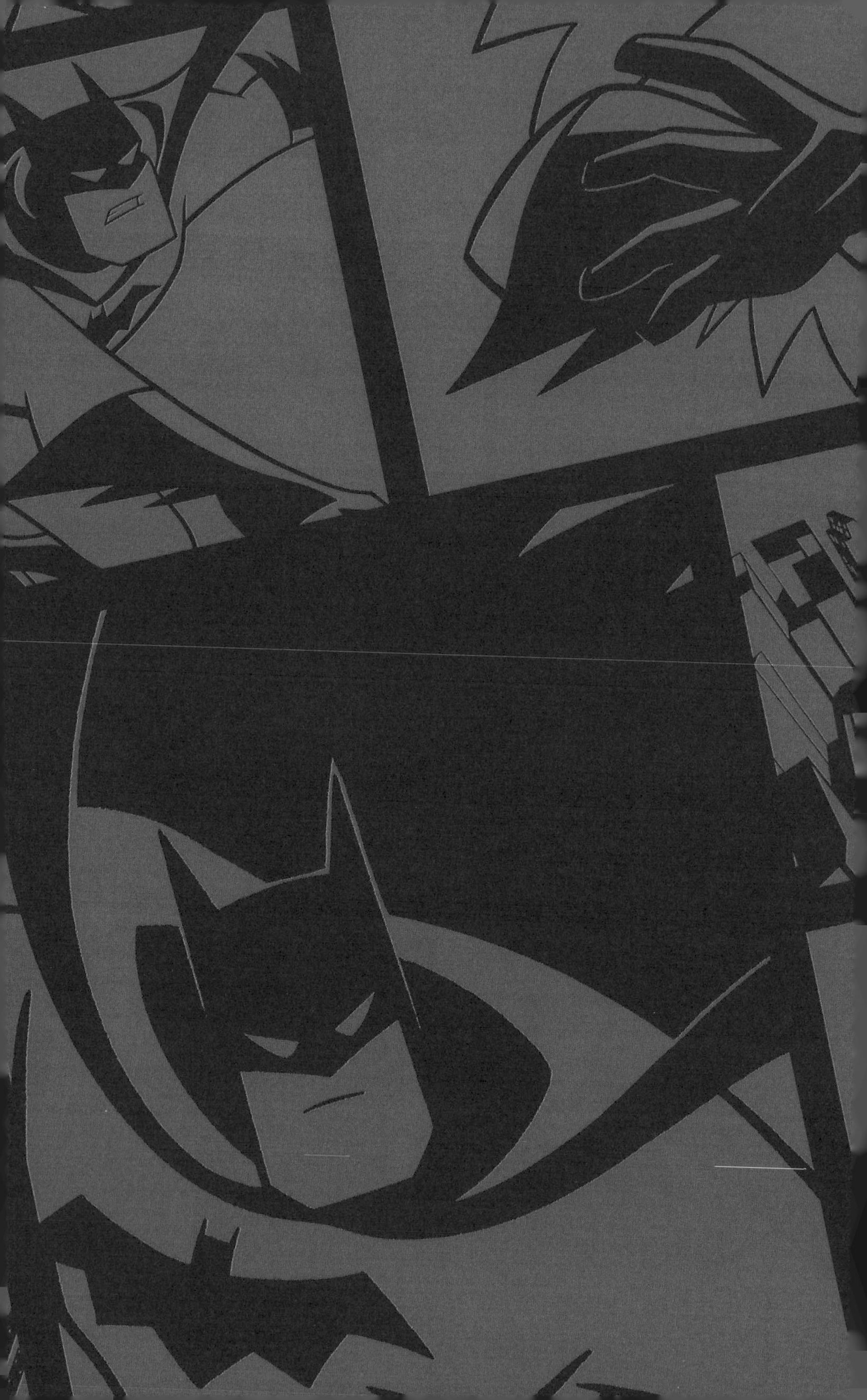

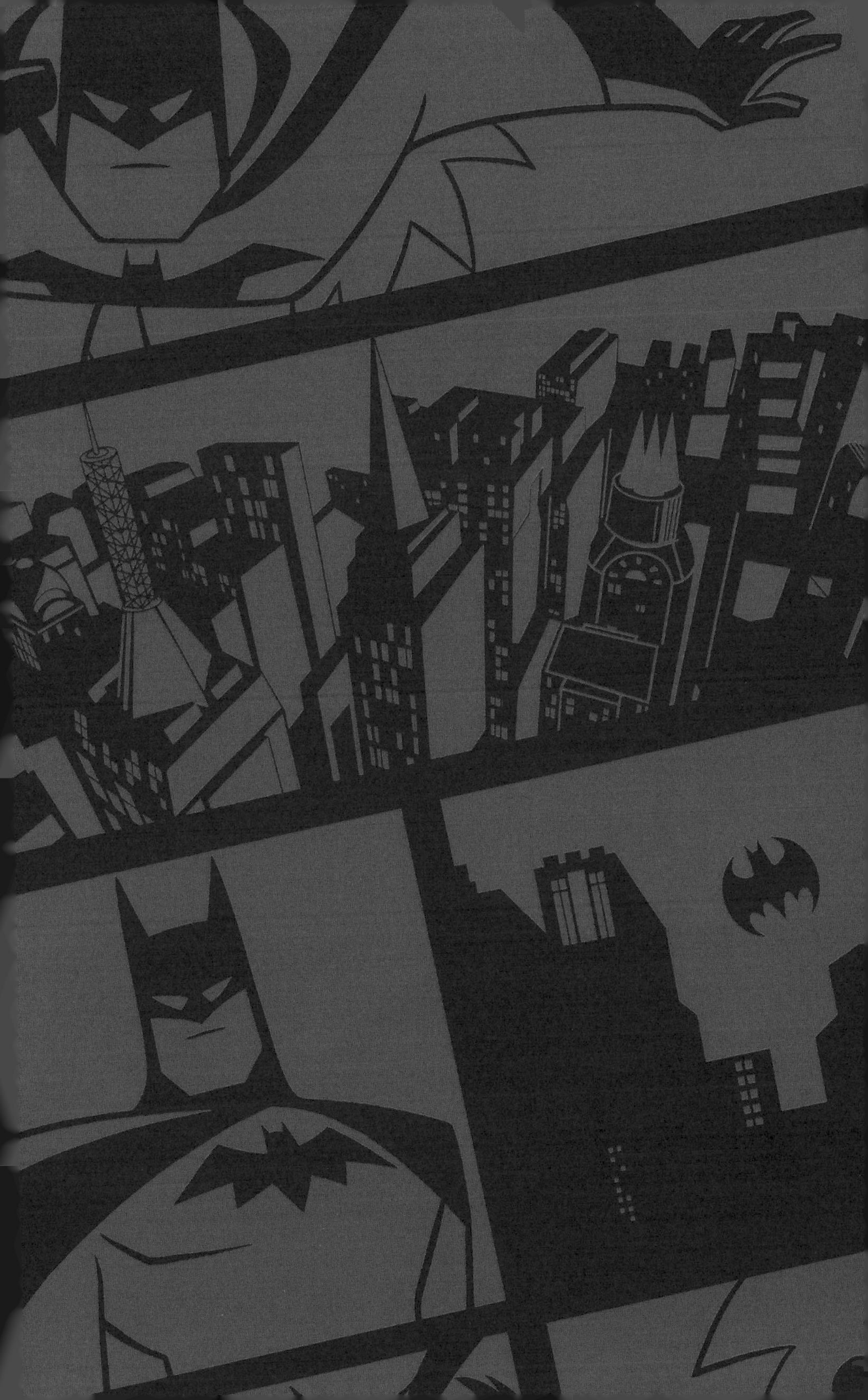

COMIC CHAPTER BOOKS

DC COMICS™
SUPER
HEROES

BATMAN™

STONE ARCH BOOKS
a capstone imprint

Batman: Comic Chapter Books are published by
Stone Arch Books,
A Capstone Imprint
1710 Roe Crest Drive
North Mankato, Minnesota 56003
www.capstoneyoungreaders.com

Star33639

Library of Congress Cataloging-in-Publication Data is
available on the Library of Congress website.

ISBN: 978-1-4965-0512-5 (library binding)
ISBN: 978-1-4965-0514-9 (paperback
ISBN: 978-1-4965-2303-7 (eBook)

Summary: The Scarecrow has fitted the Dark Knight
with a helmet that slowly gives him fear gas as part
of a twisted experiment. Batman has no choice but to
play along — the mask is tamper-proof, and if he tries
to remove it, he'll get a toxic dose of the nightmare-
inducing fumes! Will Batman outsmart the crazed villain?

Printed in Canada
052015   008825FRF15

COMIC CHAPTER BOOKS

DC COMICS™ SUPER HEROES

BATMAN™

SCARECROW'S PANIC PLOT

Batman created by Bob Kane

written by
Scott Beatty

illustrated by
Luciano Vecchio

TABLE OF CONTENTS

CHAPTER 1
SCARE TACTICS 7

CHAPTER 2
FEAR FACTORS 25

CHAPTER 3
FRIGHT FEST 39

CHAPTER 4
AVERSION THERAPY 51

CHAPTER 5
FEAR OF FLYING 61

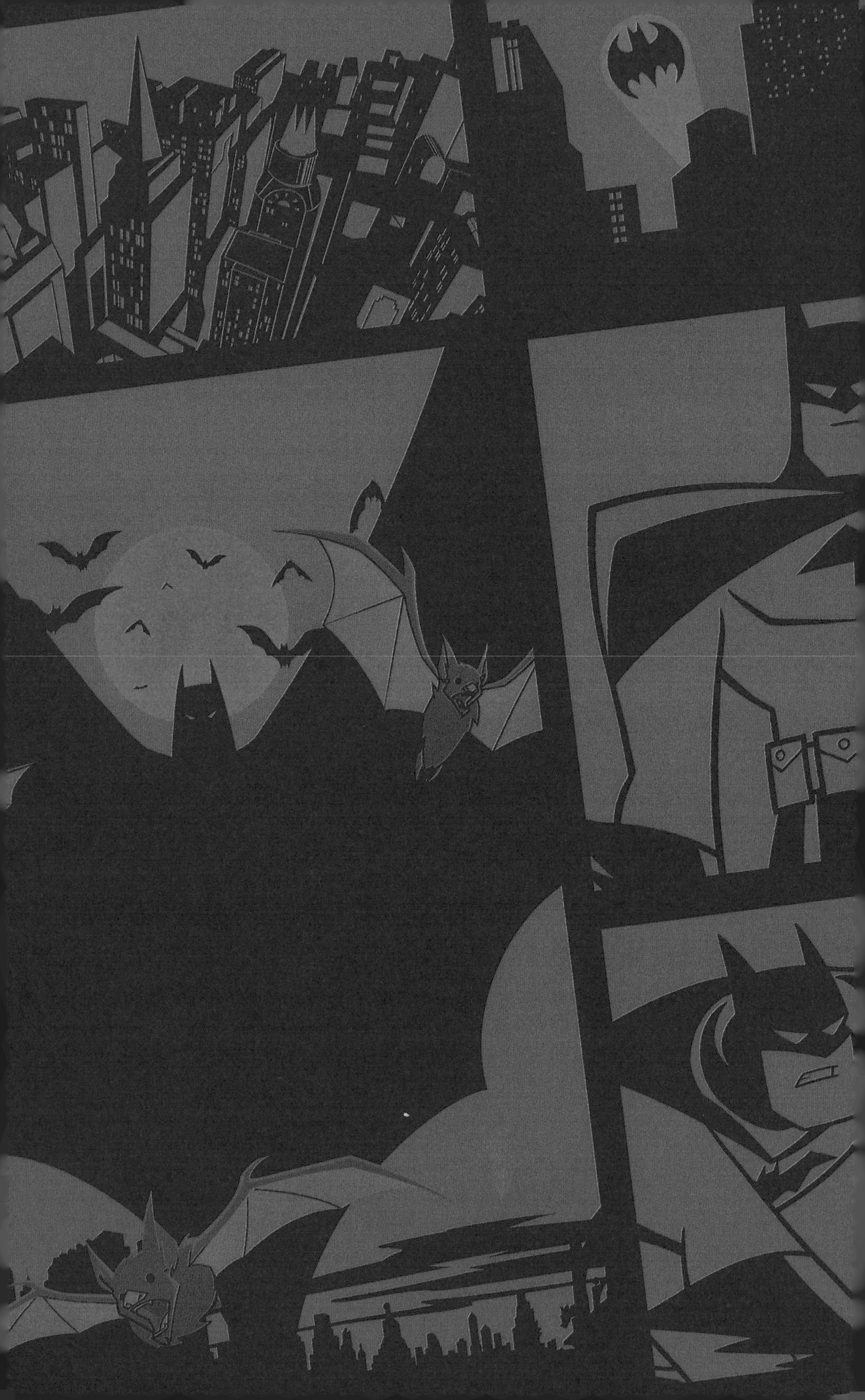

SCARE TACTICS

For Batman, work began well after nightfall when Gotham City was cloaked in darkness. That's when the worst criminals came out of their hiding places. And Batman would catch them or send them scurrying back into the shadows.

By 10:38 p.m., the Dark Knight had already thwarted a bank heist planned by the twin terrors Tweedledee and Tweedledum. He dumped the brothers, bound and gagged, at the footsteps of the Gotham City Police Department.

Then he sped off in the Batmobile in search of more troublemakers to catch.

Most nights, Batman ran without headlights. The Batmobile had an onboard crash-avoidance system very much like the sonar of his namesake, the bat. In other words, the Batmobile could steer itself, even in the dark. It also ran ultra-quiet, which gave Batman a big advantage in being able to sneak up on the bad guys.

Fifteen minutes later, Batman took a hard left.

SCREEEEEEEEEEEEEEEEEECH!

The Batmobile's tires squealed across the pavement toward Gotham Park. The park remained a mostly unspoiled woodland area that was older than the founding of the city itself. A deep, dark forest surrounded on all sides by concrete and steel canyons.

Citizens of Gotham City often went into the park during their lunch hours to escape the bustle of the city. But at night, Gotham Park was a no man's land.

The moon was full, so the park's towering trees were made more frightening in the long slats of light. Anyone who dared to travel the park's wooded labyrinth of walking and biking trails in darkness was truly brave. Or just plain crazy.

The rest that ventured in were usually out-of-towners who didn't know any better. Sometimes crooks entered the park at night to meet other criminals. And tourists and criminals are never a good mix — for obvious reasons.

Batman piloted the Batmobile along the main access road through the park. He scanned through the Batmobile's tinted canopy. On the outside, the dark material reflected the leaves rustling in the breeze. But inside, the canopy's surface displayed the heat signatures and movements of three figures just ahead.

Motion detectors and night-vision mounted in the Batmobile captured three figures just ahead. It appeared that someone was being chased by two attackers.

"Time to get back to work," Batman said.

Batman stepped hard on the Batmobile's accelerator pedal and steered onto the park's grass clearing.

VROOOOOOM!

CLUNKA-CLUNKA-CLUNK!

The vehicle's tires tore up large divots of turf as he sped toward the three figures.

"Muggers," Batman grumbled.

Of all Gotham City's criminals, he disliked muggers the most. After all, a mugger had taken his parents away when he was a young boy. Batman fought criminals every night to honor the memory of his parents.

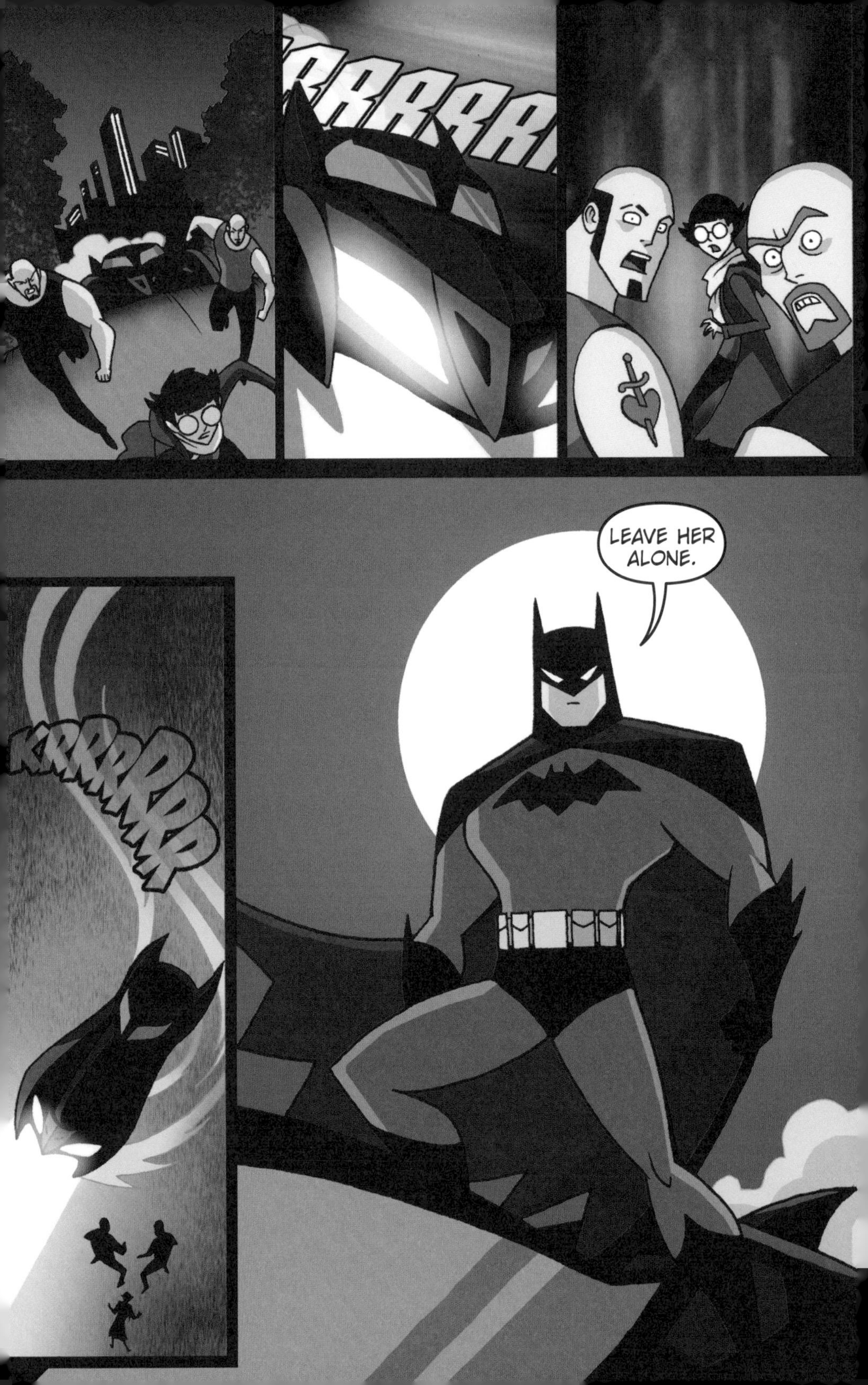
LEAVE HER ALONE.

It was a dramatic entrance. One he had practiced countless times. Once again, it had the intended effect of frightening criminals.

"B-Batman!" one of the men shouted.

THUD!

The same man went sprawling onto the grass from Batman's hard tackle. He quickly bound the man's hands and feet using rope from his Utility Belt.

The other mugger was wide-eyed like a deer in headlights. Rather than attempt to help his criminal partner, he turned and ran past the young woman.

"I'm not getting paid enough for this!" he yelled.

Batman retrieved a Batarang from his Utility Belt.

CLICK!

The Batarang unfolded into its signature shape. Batman drew back his arm, aimed, and threw. The Batarang, like a boomerang, arced through the darkness. It glinted slightly, barely visible in the park's lights shining above. But Batman could see it perfectly — special lenses in his cowl showed a special metal in the Batarang. He could track it anywhere.

The fleeing mugger, however, didn't see it coming.

THUNK!

The crook went sprawling when the Batarang struck him in the middle of his back.

The young woman watched as Batman hog-tied the second mugger's arms and legs behind his back. He carried him back to the other mugger and secured them together with another rope.

They weren't going anywhere.

Batman approached the young woman. Her back was to him and she was reaching into her handbag.

"I was so scared," she said, teary-eyed.

"You don't have to be afraid anymore," Batman said in a deep voice. He wished he could speak more softly, but it was important that he disguise his voice. No one could know that he was secretly Bruce Wayne.

The young woman turned to face Batman. She held up a skull-shaped object that Batman recognized almost immediately. She pressed a button on top of the skull.

PSSSSSSSSSST!

It sprayed a greenish gas right into Batman's face.

"No," the woman said. "Now it's YOUR turn to be afraid!"

Batman stumbled. He was dizzy and could barely focus. He fell to his knees and tried to steady himself in the damp grass, but just ended up falling over again.

"What did you do to me?" he growled.

Laughter seemed to surround him, but it wasn't coming from the young woman. It was disorienting to say the least.

"She gets an 'A' for independent study, Batman!" came a voice from behind Batman.

Batman turned to see a man emerge from a dark thicket. He was tall and gangly. He wore a threadbare sackcloth suit and hat. Over his face was a burlap mask with holes torn for his eyes and mouth.

THUD!

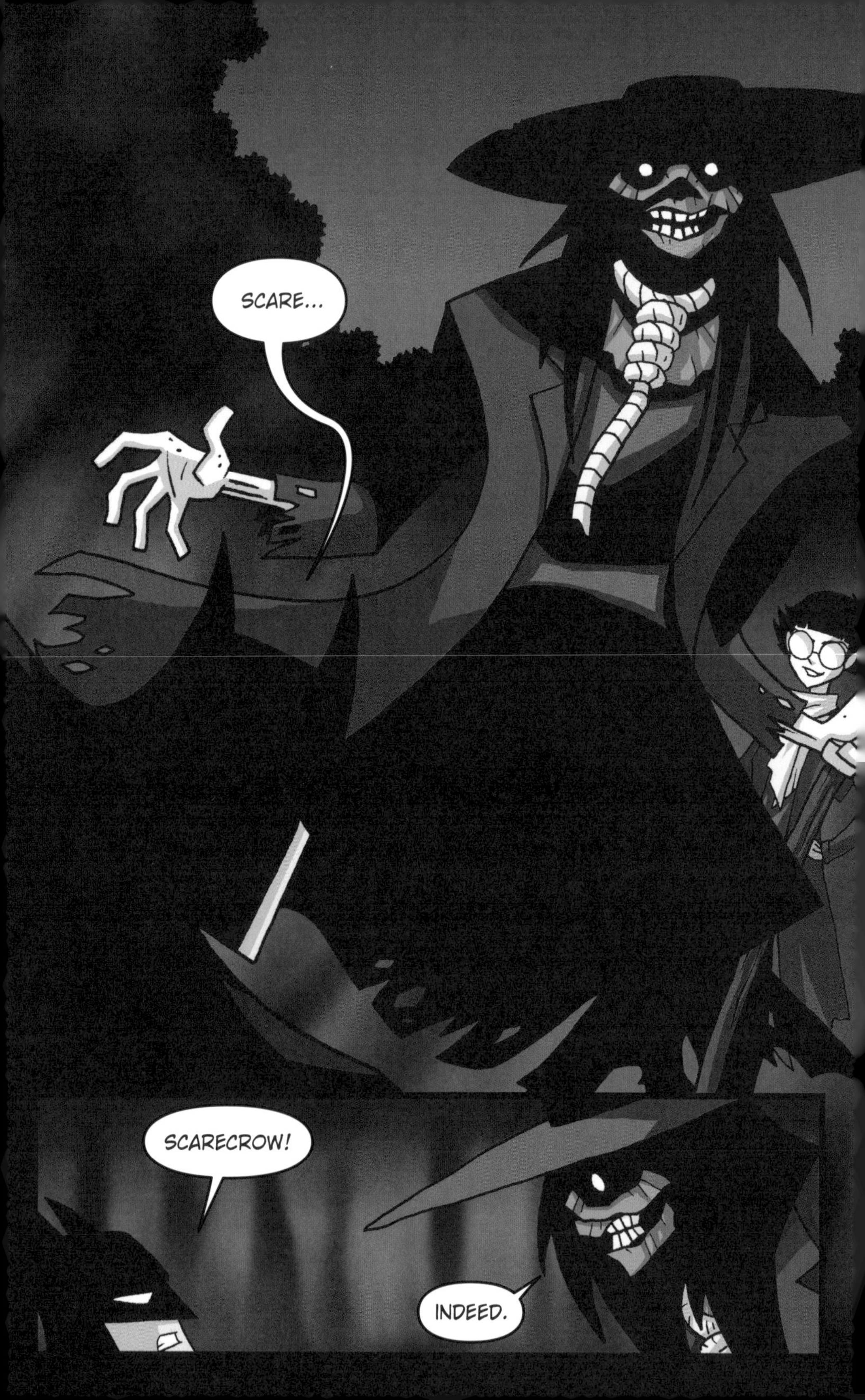
SCARE...
SCARECROW!
INDEED.

Scarecrow kicked Batman onto his back. Batman was unable to fight back. Scarecrow's fear toxin had made him as weak and timid as a kitten.

Scarecrow handed a burlap sack to the young woman. "Very nice work, Phoebe," he said. "Now let's finish the task."

"You promise you'll let me see the results of the experiment for my graduate thesis, right?" pleaded Phoebe. "You may not be a wanted criminal, but your research into fear is on the top of my most wanted list."

"Of course," said the Scarecrow. "Now be a dear and ready the Fear Helmet for our friend here, will you?"

Batman collapsed on the grass, paralyzed by fear. His struggles were useless. The toxin's effects were too strong.

Phoebe knelt next to the Dark Knight and reached to remove his cowl.

"D-don't," Batman said.

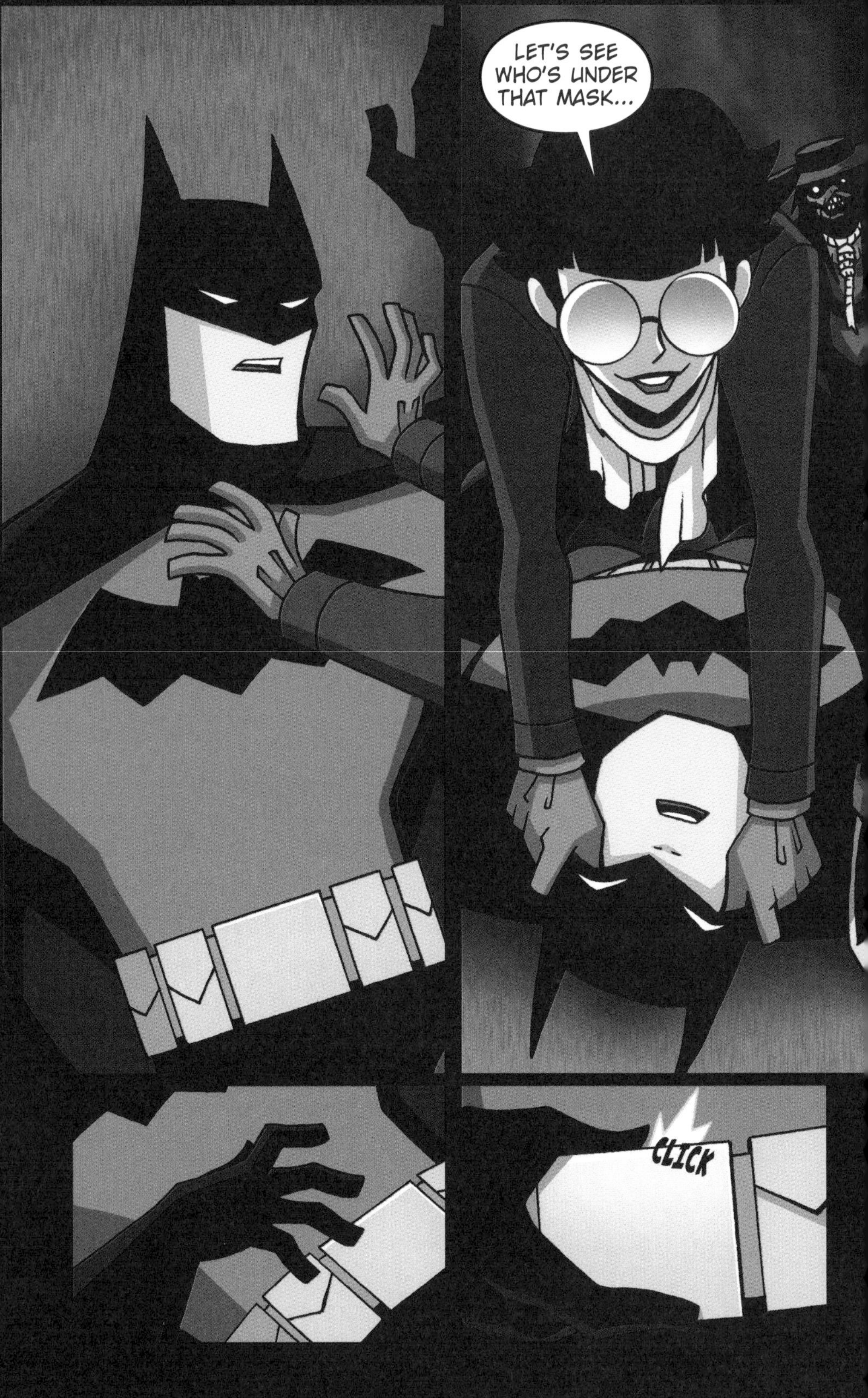
LET'S SEE WHO'S UNDER THAT MASK...
CLICK

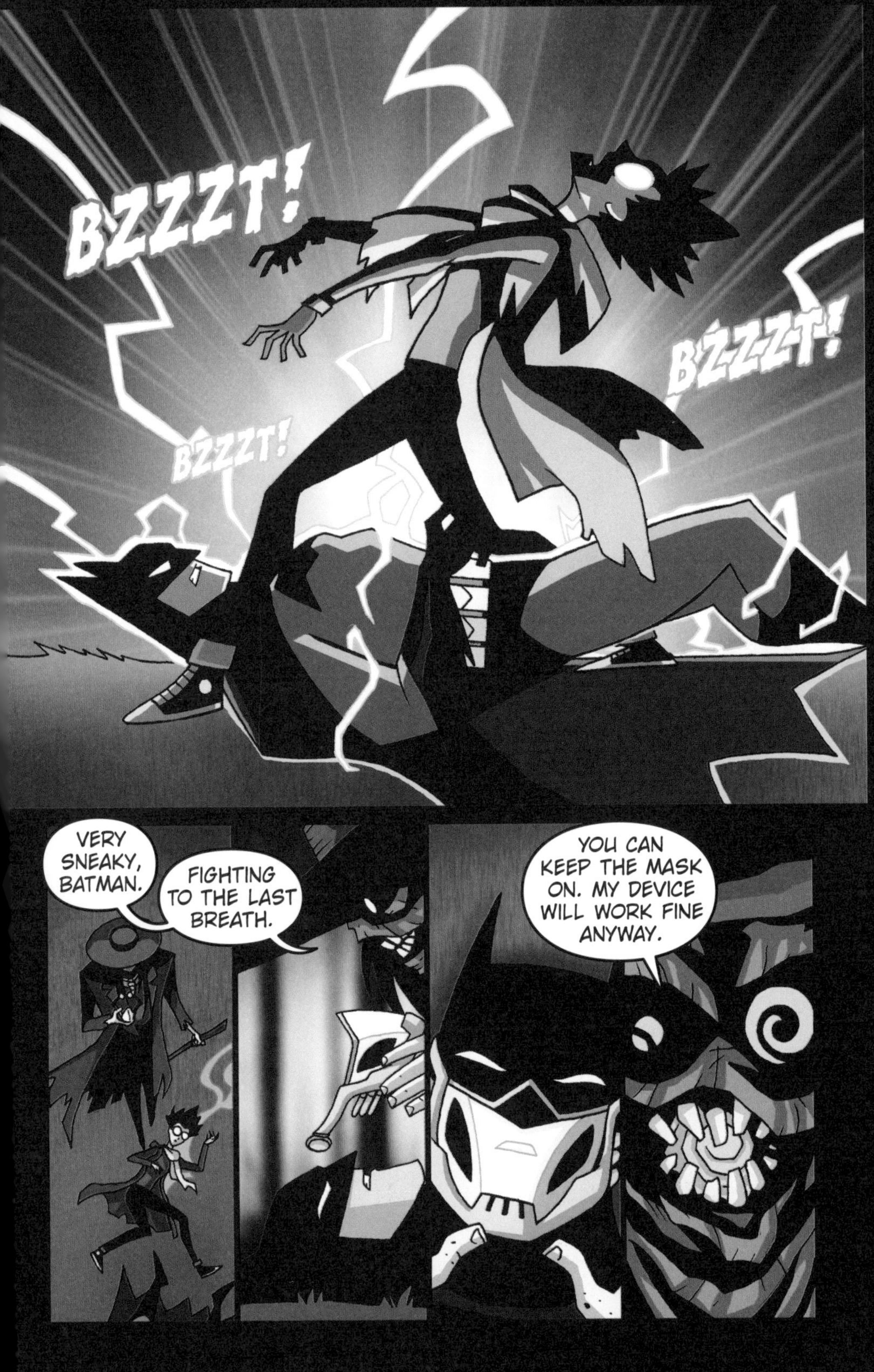
BZZZT!
BZZZT!
BZZZT!
VERY SNEAKY, BATMAN.
FIGHTING TO THE LAST BREATH.
YOU CAN KEEP THE MASK ON. MY DEVICE WILL WORK FINE ANYWAY.

If the Scarecrow had taken time to discover that Bruce Wayne was beneath Batman's cowl, then he would have also known that Bruce wasn't afraid of much. Until now, that is.

But the fight wasn't out of Batman yet. Scarecrow jumped back as the Dark Knight pushed himself to his feet. Desperately, he tried to take off the helmet that was now clamped to his head.

Scarecrow backed toward the shadow of the park's huge oak trees. "I wouldn't do that if I were you," he said.

"Why not?" Batman said. He struggled to get a good grip on the mask's locked collar.

Scarecrow held up a small remote control the size of a cell phone. "Because you've just been stricken with hylophobia," he said.

The fear-mongering felon pressed a button on his transmitter.

CLICK!

On command, one of the small canisters inside the mask released gas into Batman's nostrils and mouth.

FWOOOOOSH!

Batman tried to hold his breath, but he was eventually forced to inhale the fear toxin.

"Hylophobia?" whispered Batman.

"Yes," said Scarecrow. "The overwhelming fear of *trees!*"

Batman looked up. Withered and wrinkled faces appeared in the park's century-old oak tree trunks. They leered at him. The trees' branches seemed to reach out to grab him with giant bark-encrusted arms.

Batman shivered. Once again he struggled to remove the helmet.

"Take off the helmet and all of the canisters will be released at once," said the Scarecrow from a safe distance. "And that, Batman, would kill you."

Batman looked at the Scarecrow. The giant trees with elongated faces reached out past the villain, protecting him like a shield.

The Dark Knight did the only thing he could do. He fled.

"You can run, Batman!" cried the Scarecrow. "But you can't hide from your fears!" He cackled. "Or whatever fear I give you," he added with a smirk.

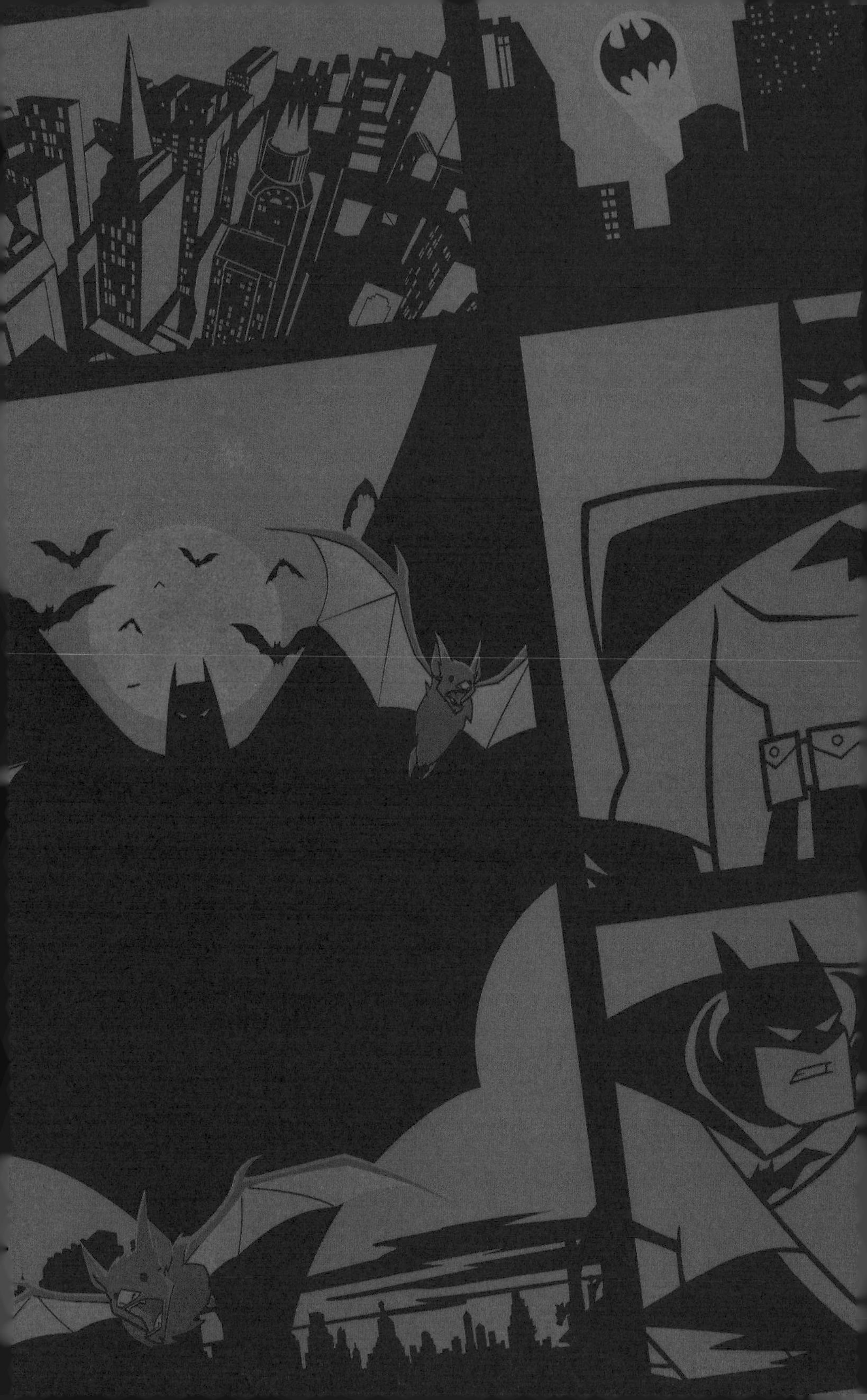

CHAPTER 2
FEAR FACTORS

MEANWHILE...

Robin, also known as the Boy Wonder, was in the Batcave. The secret area was hidden below the stately Wayne Manor, separated from the mansion by about one hundred fifty feet of limestone strata.

Robin was fighting for his life.

CLICK!

CLICK!

CLICK!

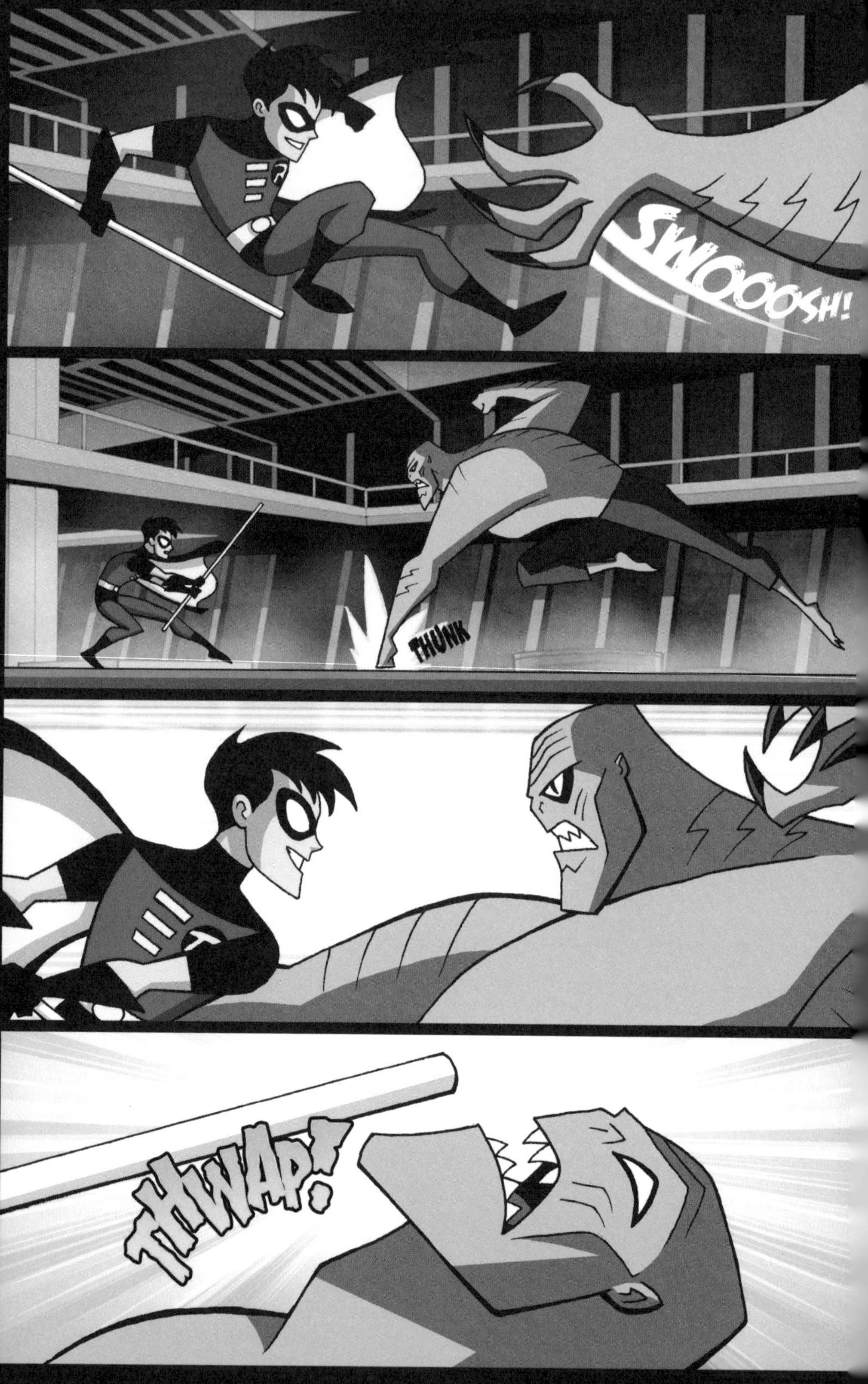
SWOOOSH!
THUNK
THWAP!

"Take *that*!" said Robin, tapping his video game controller's buttons.

On the giant display of the Batcomputer, the Boy Wonder's game character jump-kicked Killer Croc.

ZWIRT!

The villain pixilated and disintegrated from the attack.

"Do you really think that's a good use for the Batcave's computers?" came a voice from above.

Robin — Tim Drake by day — blushed as Nightwing descended the steel stairs to the Batcave's main level. The Batcomputer was state-of-the-art. It held trillions of gigabytes of information, mostly files on criminals. It also ran computer games pretty well.

Tim pushed himself back from the computer console and stood up. He was in his Robin costume except for the mask.

"Going on patrol?" asked Robin.

"Thinking about it," said Nightwing.

Without his mask and costume, Nightwing was Dick Grayson. Like Bruce, Dick lost his parents at a young age. Batman gave Dick the opportunity to bring his parents' killer to justice. Before becoming Nightwing, Dick had been Batman's first Robin. Tim became Robin after figuring out Batman's true identity. The two boys had become fast friends. They were also the Dark Knight's most trusted partners in the war on crime.

"Does Batman know you're reprogramming the Hogan's Alley simulation?" said Nightwing.

"Not yet," said Tim. "I was hoping to show him what the Batcomputer is really capable of."

REEEEE!
REEEEEEEE!

An alarm sounded and a security program overrode Tim's computer game simulation. The flat screen displayed four words that made both current and former Robin momentarily speechless: *SUIT DEFENSIVE TASER ACTIVATED*.

"Uh-oh," said Tim.

"Yup," said Dick. "Someone tried to remove Batman's mask."

Both knew this meant Batman was incapacitated — or close to it. Batman was insulated from the shock, but using it also triggered an alarm in the Batcomputer. That meant Batman likely needed the help that only a trusted sidekick or two could provide.

Nightwing sprinted to the fleet of vehicles parked in the Batcave's garage. He donned a motorcycle helmet with the same blue and black coloring as his costume.

Nightwing turned to call back to Tim, "Lock in his location with GPS and keep me updated on his movement while I'm gone!"

But Tim was already next to him, mask in place, wearing his own helmet. Tim produced a handheld tablet linked to the Batcomputer. He jerked his thumb at a nearby Batcycle with a sidecar attached.

"If Batman is in trouble," Tim said, "I should be along for the ride."

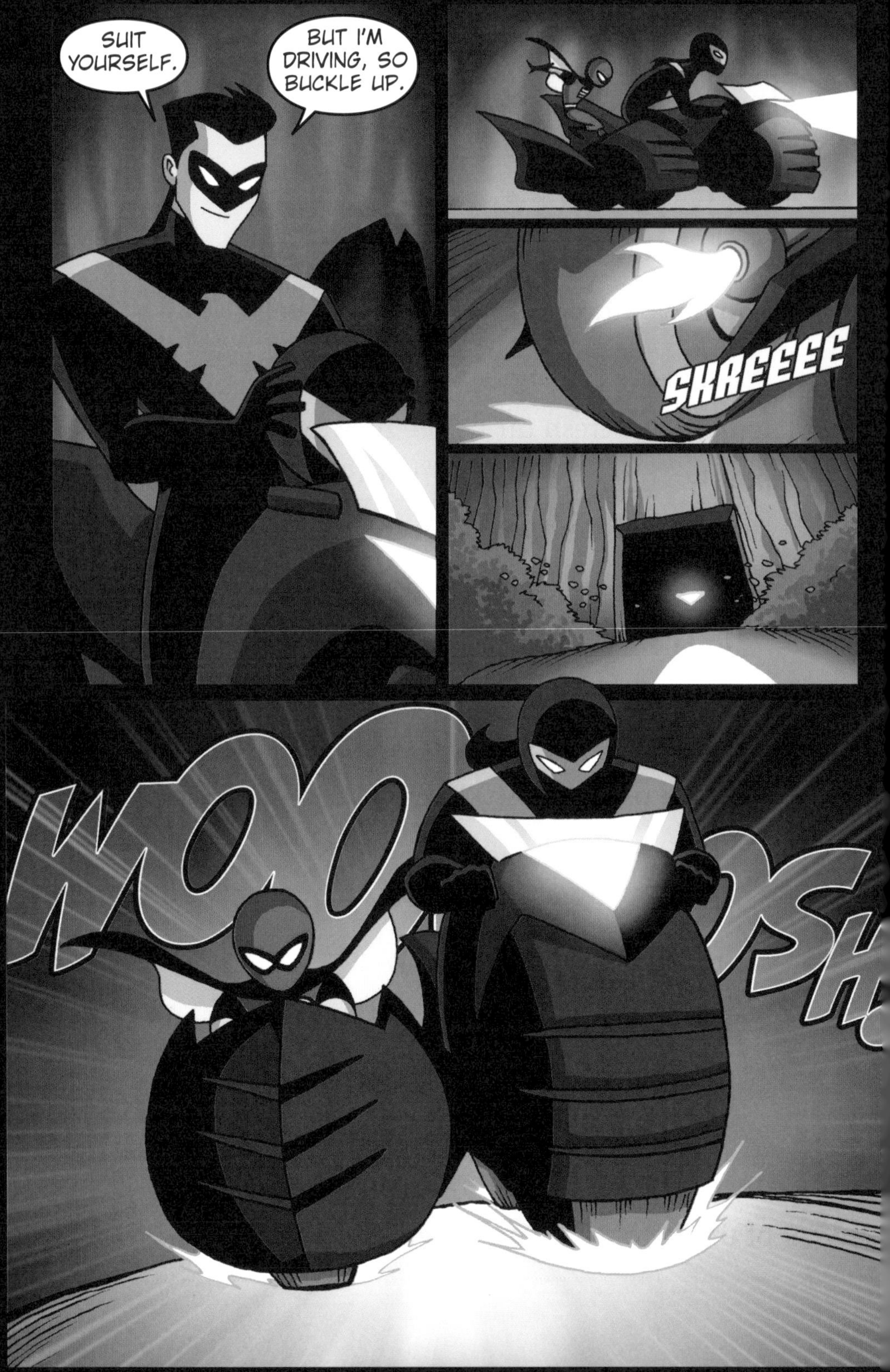
SUIT YOURSELF.
BUT I'M DRIVING, SO BUCKLE UP.
SKREEEE
WOOOOSH

MEANWHILE, BACK AT GOTHAM PARK...

Batman stopped running. He took out another Batarang from his Utility Belt.

The Fear Gas made him confused. He had to get some fresh air before he was completely paralyzed with fright. To do so, he needed to free himself from the Scarecrow's Fear Mask.

CLICK!

The Batarang snapped open. Batman used the edge of it to bash the mask's transparent bubble.

CLUD! CLUD! CLUD!

Each blow was harder than the last. The sound inside the helmet was deafening, even under Batman's cowl. But the toughened alloy of the Batarang didn't even scratch the mask.

"I wouldn't do that if I were you!" shouted the Scarecrow.

The villain was out of breath from struggling to keep up with the Dark Knight. Even incapacitated with fear toxin, Batman was a superior athlete to the gangly Jonathan Crane.

Batman spun around and saw the Scarecrow holding his remote control.

"There are micro-cameras in the helmet, Batman!" he said. "You can't escape me that easily."

Batman gripped the Batarang tightly.

"And besides," the Scarecrow said gleefully, "I've rigged my Fear Mask to release the full amount of fear toxin if you so much as try to remove it! So you'll have to play out my little experiment and suffer one fear at a time, or risk being exposed to EVERY fear you can possibly imagine all at once!"

Batman let the Scarecrow babble. He had discovered in his many years of fighting crime that villains loved to talk about their evil plans.

They wanted nothing more than respect for their well-planned schemes. For Batman, these lectures often gave him precious moments to escape — or to prepare a counter-attack and save the day.

Batman hurled the Batarang at the Scarecrow.

The Scarecrow, however, wasn't slowed by fear toxin like Batman was. He ducked the weapon's arcing path.

WOOOSH!

As he did, Scarecrow activated the remote control. Inside the Fear Mask, Batman was dosed with more fear toxin. The Dark Knight choked and sputtered. He reached out to catch the returning Batarang, but all he could see was a swarm of bats!

FLAP-FLAP-FLAP! Large and small ones beat their leathery wings as they descended on him.

"The bat was your symbol of fear!" said the Scarecrow. "Now it is your weakness. Suffer from chiroptophobia, a fear of bats!"

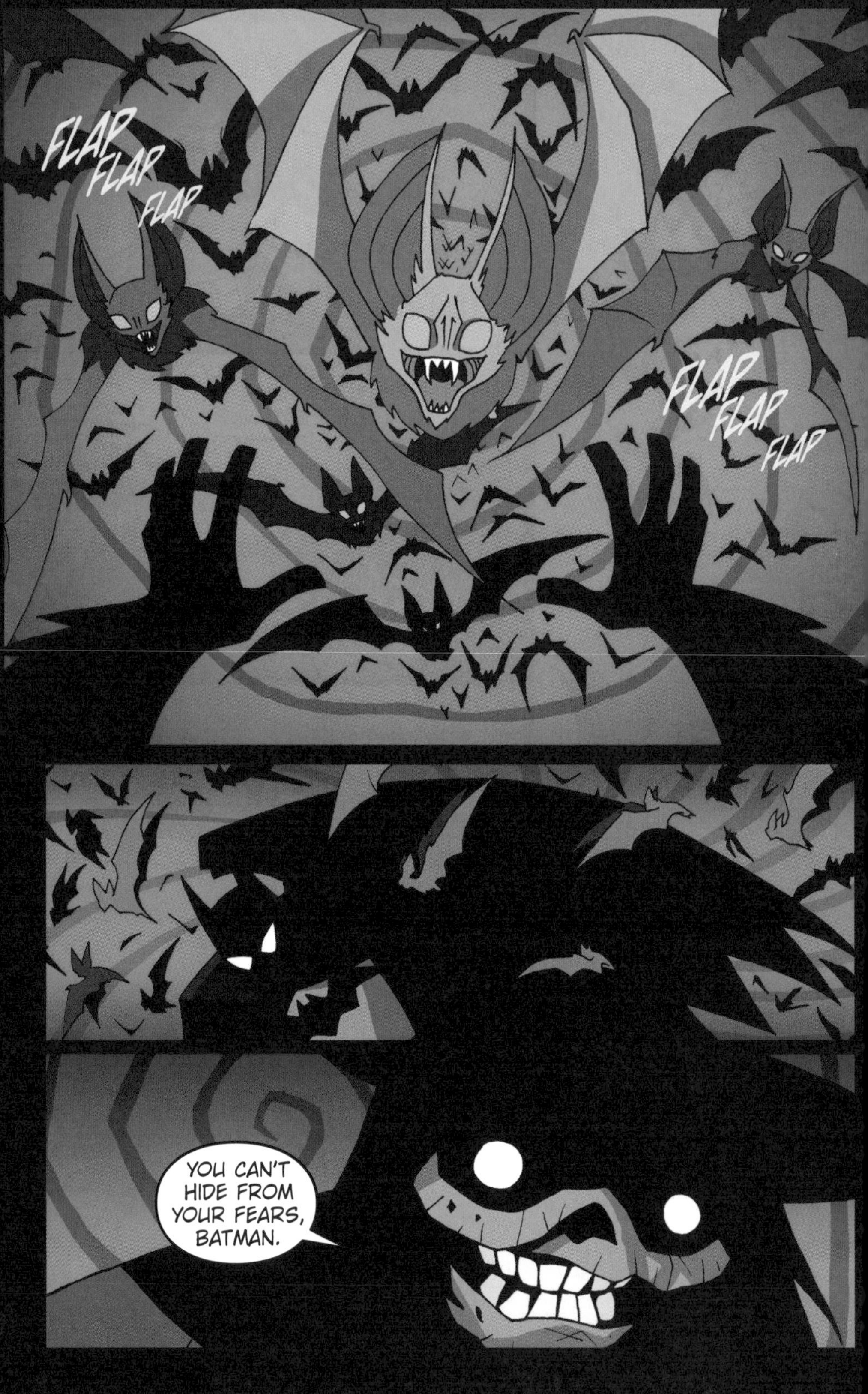
FLAP FLAP FLAP
FLAP FLAP FLAP
YOU CAN'T HIDE FROM YOUR FEARS, BATMAN.

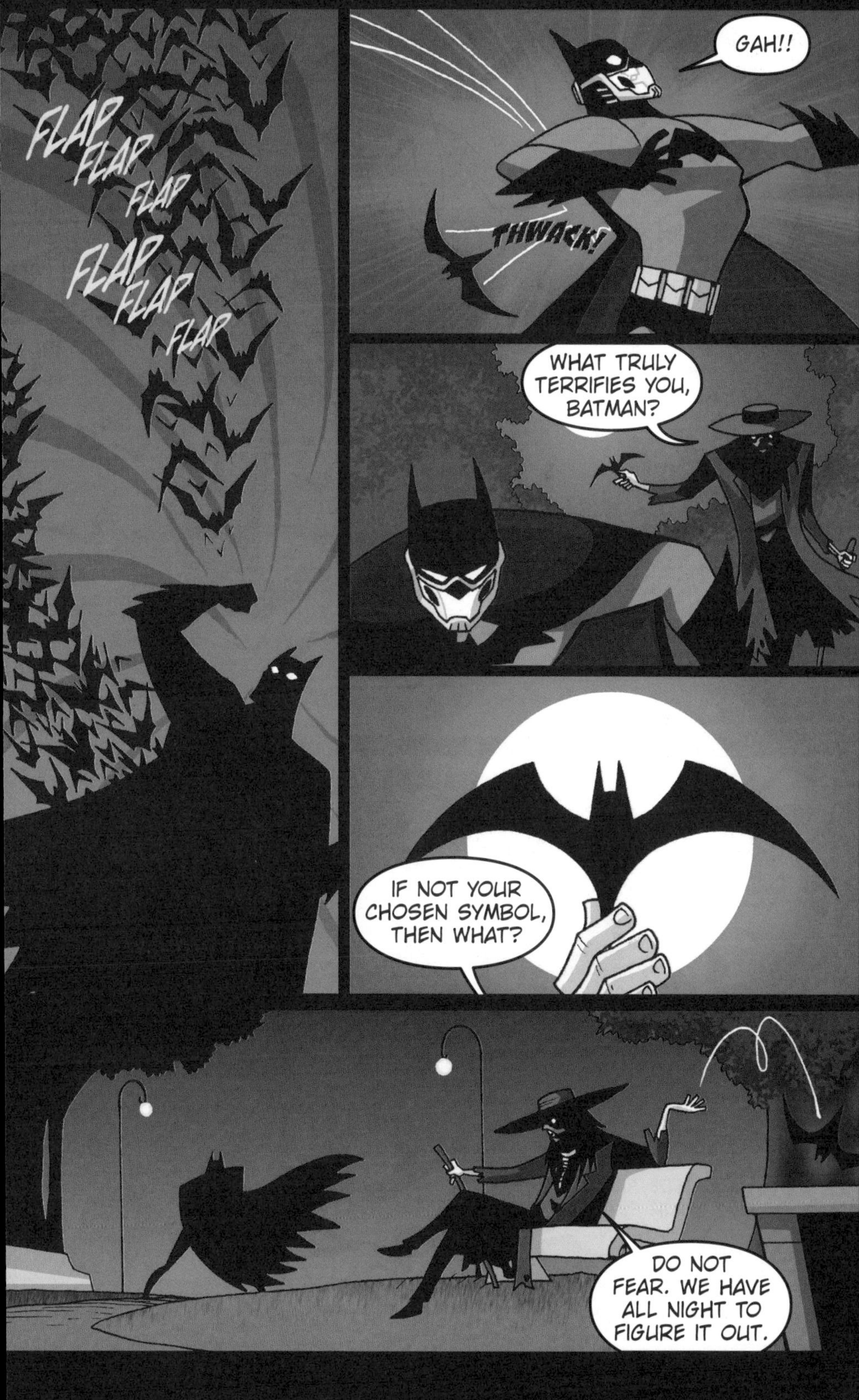
FLAP
FLAP
FLAP
FLAP
FLAP
FLAP
GAH!!
THWACK!
WHAT TRULY TERRIFIES YOU, BATMAN?
IF NOT YOUR CHOSEN SYMBOL, THEN WHAT?
DO NOT FEAR. WE HAVE ALL NIGHT TO FIGURE IT OUT.

The road from Wayne Manor to Gotham City was mostly private. Bruce Wayne owned the majority of the land between his mansion and the city limits. So there were no state or local police waiting behind shrubs to catch speeders.

Nightwing throttled up on the Batcycle's accelerator. The bike zoomed faster. Robin held on for dear life, one hand on the sidecar, the other focused on the tablet. Onscreen, a small bat-shaped icon showed Batman's location. He was headed out of Gotham Park toward the Upper East Side.

"He's on the move!" shouted Robin over the roar of the Batcycle and the whipping wind. "He must be okay!"

"Not necessarily!" shouted Nightwing. "This is Gotham City, remember!"

Robin nodded grimly. In Gotham City, especially at night when the criminals crawled

out from under their rocks, anything was
possible.

ZWOOOOOOM!

Nightwing pushed the Batcycle to its limit.
Robin held on tighter.

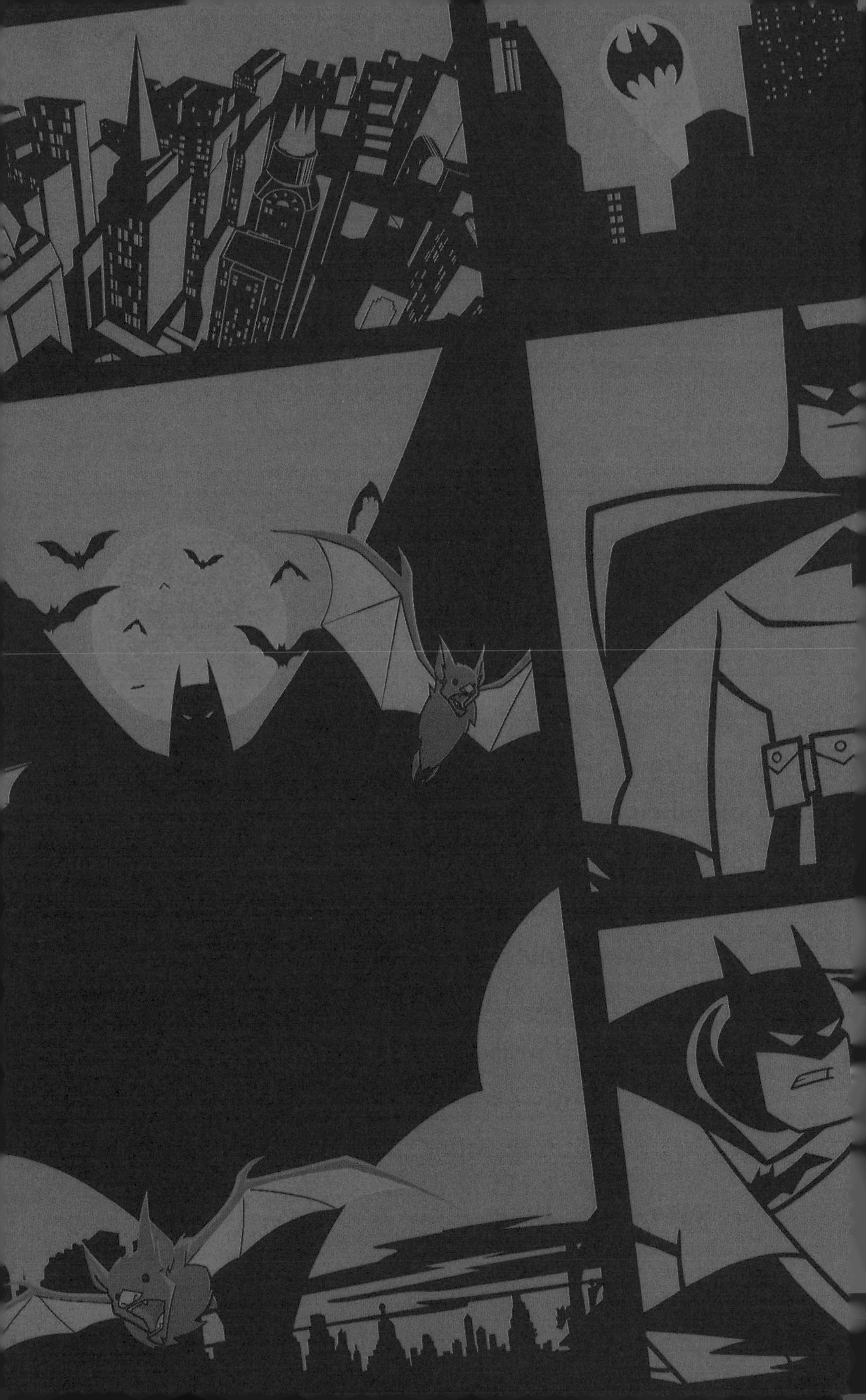

CHAPTER 3
FRIGHT FEST

Batman had experienced the Scarecrow's fear toxin before. He had worked hard to build up a tolerance to the effects of it by giving himself small doses to adapt. He got the idea from the way snake handlers would inject small doses of snake venom into their bodies so their bodies would build up resistance to it over time. It wasn't immunity exactly, but it did protect them, and Batman, from the worst of it.

But not this time.

Scarecrow operated the Fear Mask by remote control. Batman assumed it had to have a limited effective range. So he ran, not out of fear as the Scarecrow likely assumed, but to put as much distance between the mask and the controller as possible.

Batman paused next to a pond. If he dived down deep enough, maybe the Fear Mask would short-circuit. *Or it might release a full dose and suffocate me at the same time,* Batman thought.

The mask's collar prevented him from touching the earpiece in his cowl to signal the Batcave for help. "I'm on my own," he said aloud.

FZZZT!

A tiny speaker within the helmet crackled. "No, Batman, you're not," said Scarecrow.

Batman looked at the pond again. It might be worth a try.

"Do you suffer aquaphobia, Caped Crusader?" Scarecrow said. "It's an overwhelming fear of water and drowning."

A gas canister within the Fear Mask sprayed Batman with its contents. The Dark Knight blinked to clear his eyes and looked at the pond. Now it seemed to stretch out forever like a great ocean. He blinked again and the ripples in the water turned into whirlpools. Lapping waves threatened to suck him into the watery abyss.

"Better head to higher ground if you suffer such a phobia!" said the Scarecrow's voice from the helmet's speaker.

Batman took the advice and ran in the opposite direction. A moment later, he exited the park into Gotham City's maze of concrete and steel.

MEANWHILE...

"Stop, stop, STOP!" Robin said.

Nightwing braked hard and the Batcycle lurched to a halt. Its rear tire and the sidecar briefly lifted off the asphalt. Robin was furiously tapping on the tablet to open apps and windows. One mini-screen showed the bat icon tracking Batman's path through the streets.

"Listen to this!" said Robin. He patched the audio into their own helmets' audio systems.

Nightwing's jaw clenched as he heard the Scarecrow's voice taunting Batman.

"Better head to higher ground if you suffer such a phobia!" repeated the recording.

"What? How are you doing this?" said Nightwing.

"I hacked into Batman's cowl receiver," said Robin.

"And he's having a conversation with the Scarecrow?" asked Nightwing.

"I don't think so," said Robin gravely. "I think the Scarecrow's controlling him."

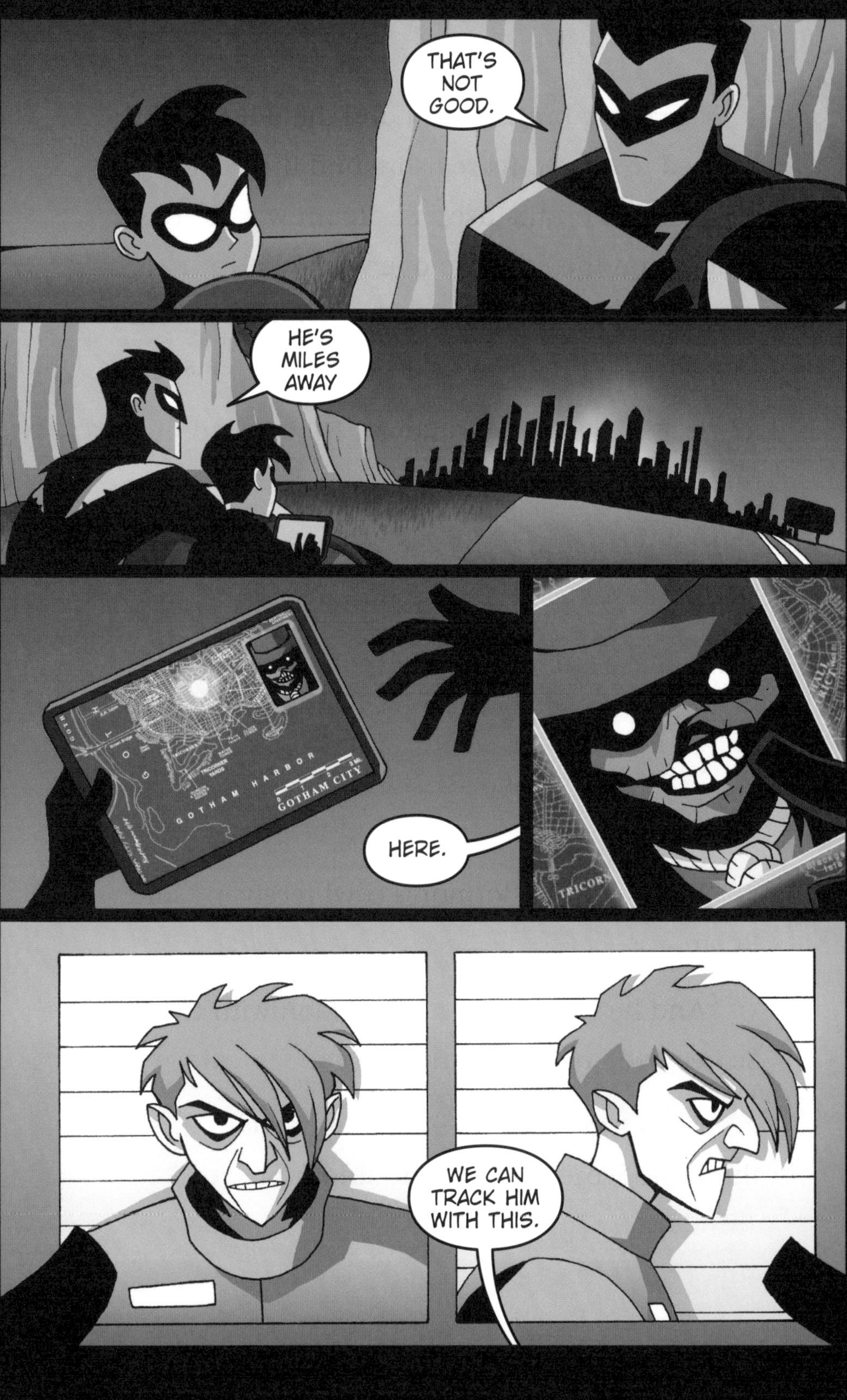
THAT'S NOT GOOD.
HE'S MILES AWAY
GOTHAM HARBOR
GOTHAM CITY
HERE.
WE CAN TRACK HIM WITH THIS.

Nightwing glared at the image of the villain. "Scarecrow does enjoy mind games," he said. "Run it back again. Play everything you recorded from the start. We need to know everything. Where's Batman now?"

AT THE SAME TIME...

Visitors to Gotham Park often took advantage of the city's free zoo. It boasted a collection of many exotic animals. The Wayne Foundation charity kept the zoo's animals fed and its keepers paid.

Batman needed a moment to rest and figure things out, so he vaulted the gate and ran into the zoo's central square. Huge sculptures of various cartoon animals greeted him. Each pointed the way to a different species' cage or habitat.

"Not so clever, Batman," said Scarecrow through the cowl's radio. "Animal phobias are among the most common and numerous!"

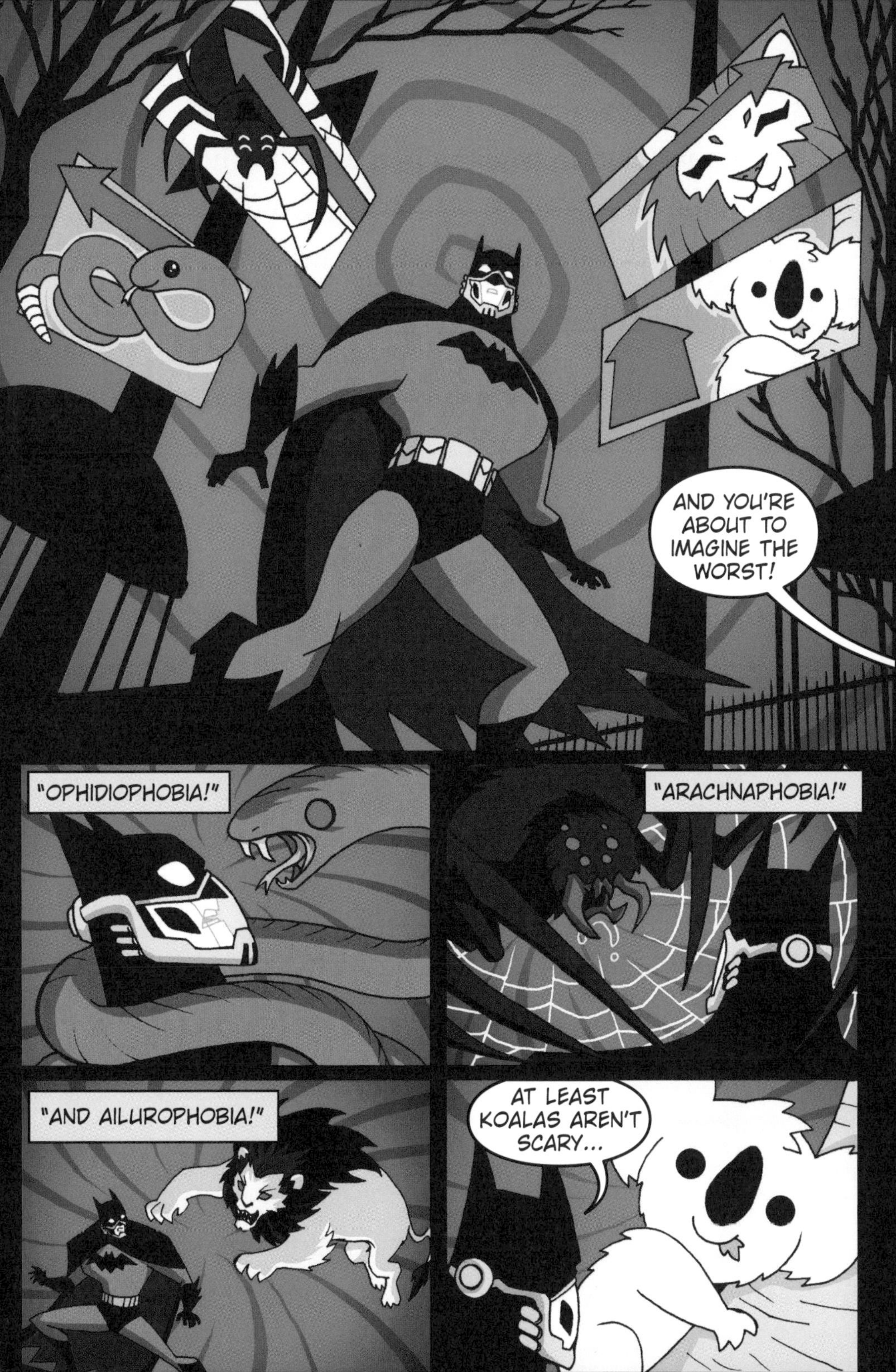

AND YOU'RE ABOUT TO IMAGINE THE WORST!
"OPHIDIOPHOBIA!"
"ARACHNAPHOBIA!"
"AND AILUROPHOBIA!"
AT LEAST KOALAS AREN'T SCARY...

Batman closed his eyes tightly. If he couldn't see anything, maybe the fear toxin wouldn't be as effective.

"The gas is a hallucinogen," Scarecrow said. "You see what you imagine!"

It was like Scarecrow could read Batman's thoughts . . . or see him through the device.

Batman blinked again, waiting. The koala didn't transform into a monstrous version of itself. It merely stared at the Caped Crusader and munched on its eucalyptus leaves.

"That one isn't in your Fear Book, is it, Scarecrow?" said Batman. "There's no documented fear of koala bears, is there?"

He didn't wait for a response. He sidestepped the giant skittering spider and leaped over the slithering snake.

ROAR!

Batman vaulted over the lion and headed for the zoo's exit.

The Scarecrow, meanwhile, was beside himself with rage. "There's a phobia for everything!" he roared.

The villain sat back in the seat of his car and drummed his burlap-gloved fingers on the steering wheel. His vehicle wasn't as exotic as the Batmobile. It had no hidden weapons or a superpowered engine.

In fact, it was Phoebe's rental car, the young woman who was awakening from her taser shock in the middle of the park about now. Scarecrow needed the car to stay close to Batman. The experiment wasn't over. It was 12:45 a.m.

The night was still young.

"Dr. Crane?" came a voice from the radio.

The Scarecrow nearly jumped out of his own frightful costume when the remote control on the passenger seat spoke to him. It wasn't Batman's voice he heard.

"Dr. Crane, we know what you're doing," said Robin.

The Scarecrow felt his heart beat faster. A chill ran down his spine.

MEANWHILE...

The Batcycle sped across a bridge into Gotham City. Nightwing focused on the road ahead, weaving in and out of late night drivers. Robin tracked Batman's movements through the city and pointed for Nightwing to take the first exit ramp.

"Not only do we know what you're doing, Dr. Crane," said Robin, "but we know how we're going to stop you."

Robin tapped a button on the tablet screen and muted the transmission.

Nightwing glanced at Robin. "We do?" said Nightwing.

"I have a few ideas. We'll start with reverse psychology," said Robin.

Nightwing nodded. Tim Drake was gifted in many things, including criminal psychology and computers. If Tim said he knew the answer, he did.

Besides, Nightwing thought. *If Tim didn't, then Batman doesn't stand a chance.*

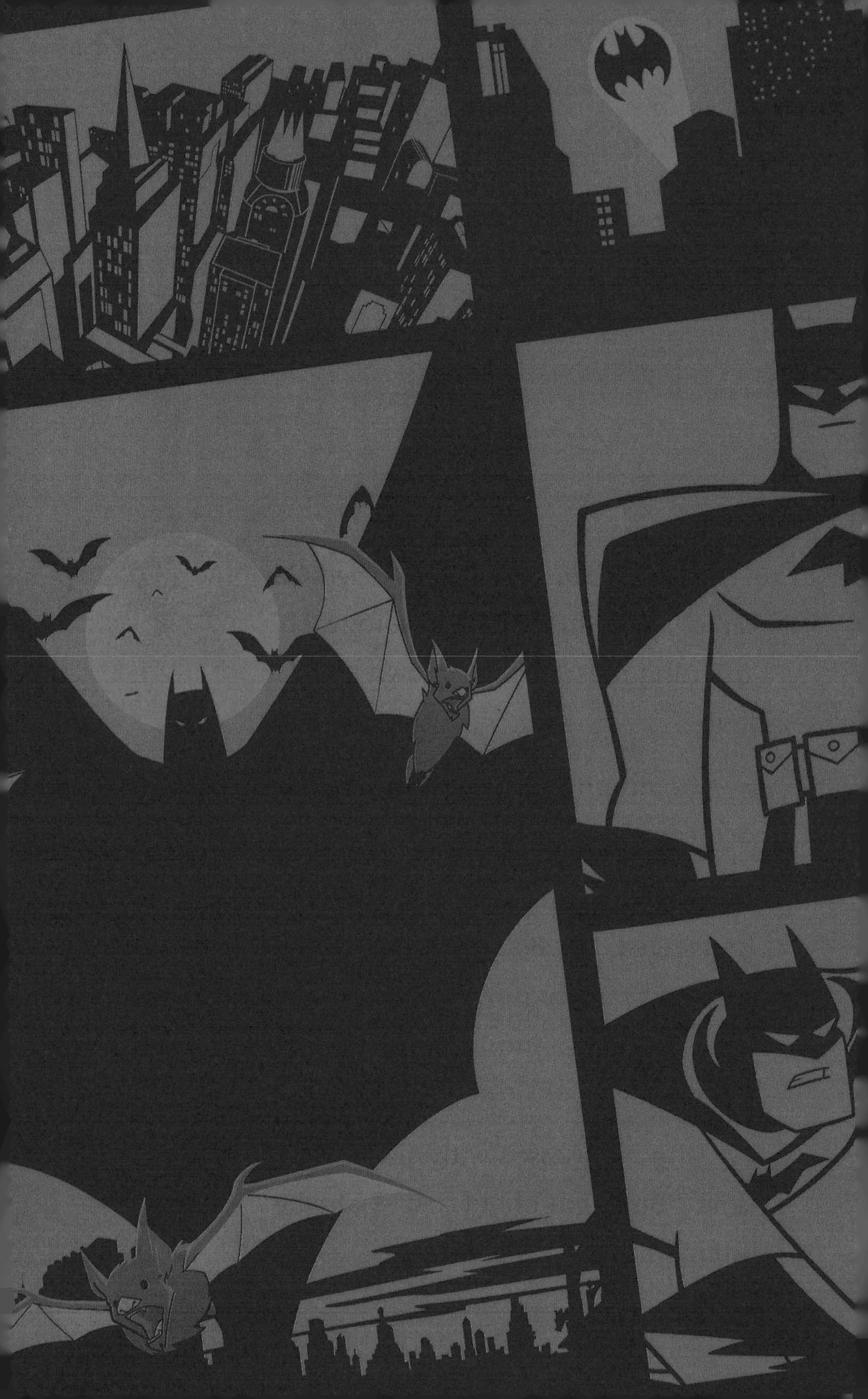

CHAPTER 4

AVERSION THERAPY

Batman ran down a darkened Gotham City street past a fast food restaurant. The diner's grinning mascot was a clown with multi-colored hair.

"Coulrophobia is a fear of clowns," Scarecrow said. "Did you know that?!"

The Fear Helmet spritzed again and Batman shuddered. But Batman kept running. He'd fought a particular clown many times before, and this diner's mascot hardly compared to the Clown Prince of Crime.

"You're obsessed with my fears," Batman said. "But what about yours? Maybe . . . nomophobia?

Scarecrow gasped. "Fear of losing cell phone contact?" he said. The villain stamped hard on his rental car's gas pedal.

RUMBLE! The tiny sedan lurched forward and clipped a fire hydrant.

WOOOOOSH!

A geyser from the broken hydrant sprayed into the air.

AT THE SAME TIME...

Batman lurched down the street past a clothing shop. Inside, beautiful mannequins modeled the latest fashions. They gazed at Batman with unblinking eyes. Batman hesitated.

Scarecrow took advantage of the Dark Knight's pause. "Pediophobia! Fear of mannequins!" he said through the Fear Mask.

Batman blinked — and the mannequins came to life!

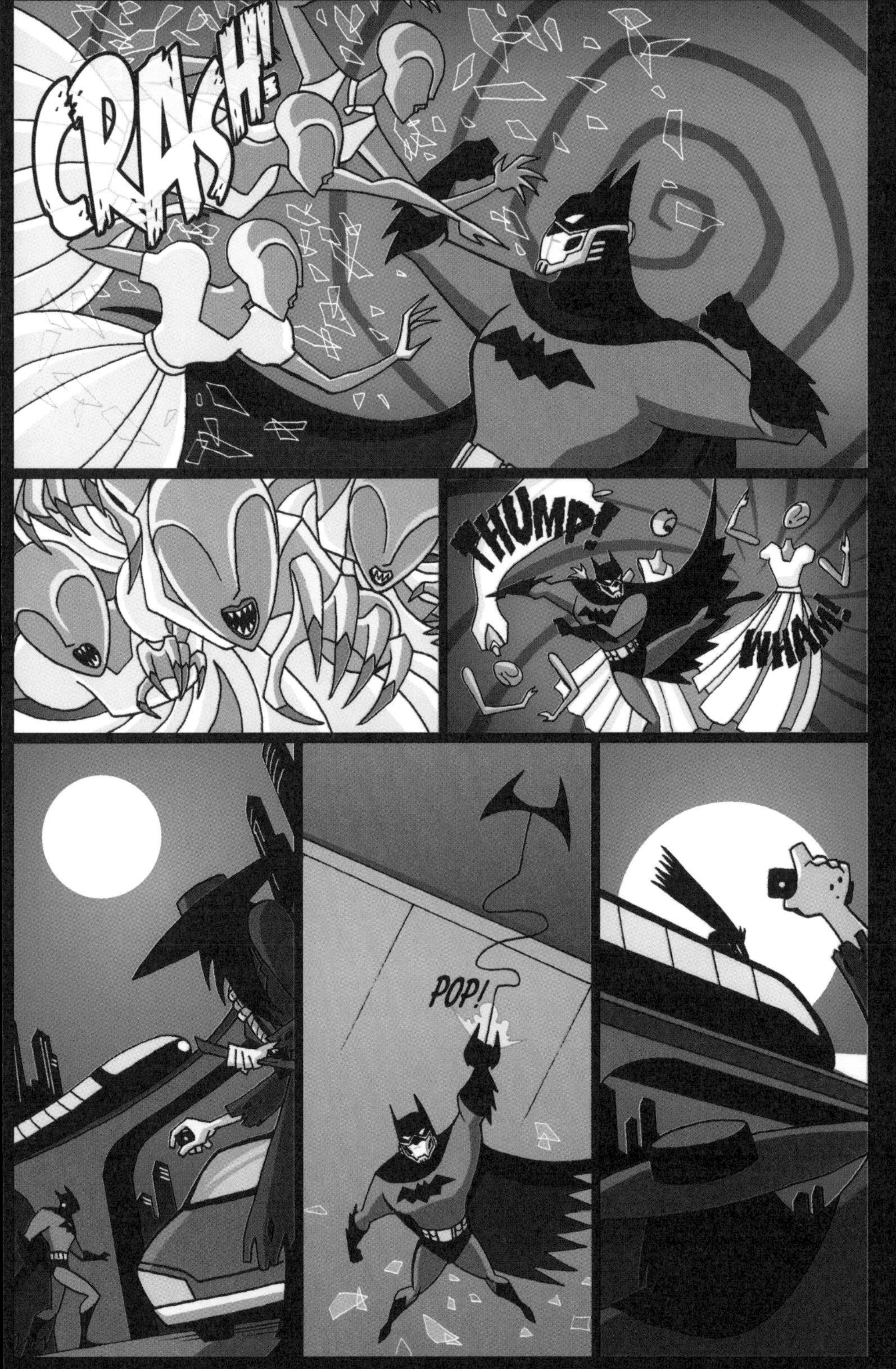
CRASH!
THUMP!
WHAM!
POP!

"Turn here!" yelled Robin over the roar of the Batcycle's engine.

Nightwing twisted hard on the handlebars. The Batcycle raced past a street flooded with water from a broken hydrant.

SWISH!

SHREEEEEEEEEE!

Nightwing made a hard turn and braked hard. From behind the geyser of water flooding the street, they saw the Scarecrow trying to climb back into his rental car.

"Where's Batman?" said Nightwing.

Robin pointed to the tablet. The bat icon was hurrying out of the frame on a straight-line path atop the monorail's route.

"He's on the train!" cried Robin.

"You take Scarecrow! Get that transmitter! I'm going after Batman!" said Nightwing. He gunned the Batcycle throttle as Robin leaped out.

Batman clawed his way to the top of the train. He lay atop it, exhausted from the night's terrors. The cool rush of air from the train's speedy progress was some comfort. At least until Scarecrow spoke.

"Do you know what the fear of trains is called, Batman?" Scarecrow asked.

Batman closed his eyes. He did know. After fighting the Scarecrow for years, he had studied up on every known fear and phobia. He knew the best way to combat most criminals was with knowledge.

"Siderodromophobia," said Batman through gritted teeth.

The Fear Mask sprayed him once more.

"HAHAHAHAHAHA!" Scarecrow laughed.

As he did, Robin took the opportunity to sneak up behind him.

"How about ornithophobia?" Robin said. "I wonder: can a scarecrow be afraid of birds, even if it's supposed to be the other way around?"

Scarecrow spun around and the Boy Wonder smacked him with his bo staff.

THUNK!

The villain fell to his knees. Robin lifted his staff and brought it down hard on the remote control.

CRUNCH!

FZZZZZZT!

The remote control's casing cracked and the transmitter let out sparks.

ATOP THE TRAIN...

Batman held on for dear life. In his mind, the train had jumped its normal track and was bucking like a bronco. It followed a spiraling and gravity-defying track like an unsafe roller coaster.

Though it was only an illusion, the effect on Batman was real. If he lost his grip he would fall to his doom . . . and his fingers were getting tired.

Far below, Nightwing was starting to catch up with the train. He could see that Batman was battling unseen demons. He had to do something to help his mentor — and FAST.

With his gloved thumb, Nightwing activated

the Batcycle's autopilot. The bike remained in constant speed to match the monorail's speed.

He crouched atop the Batcycle's seat, took a deep breath, and leapt onto the train!

WOOOOOSSSHH!

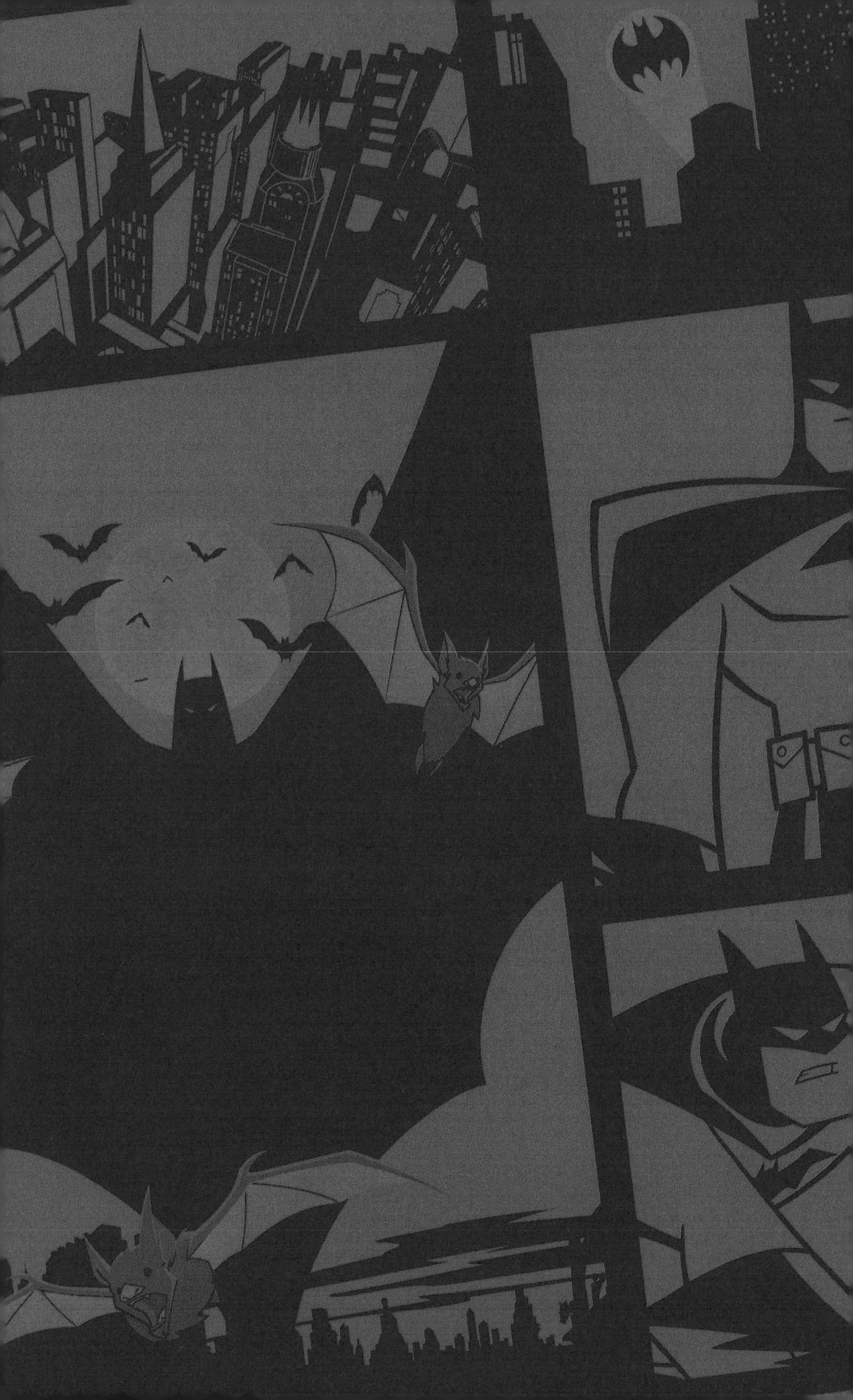

CHAPTER 5

FEAR OF FLYING

It was hard going, especially with the monorail moving at maximum speed, but Nightwing was able to pull himself up and atop it.

Three cars away, Batman was cowering in fear. He could barely move.

"It's going to be all right!" Nightwing called to him.

Batman wanted to believe it. He'd never given up before. And he wouldn't now.

Many blocks away, behind the train's path, Scarecrow refused to give up, too.

THUD!

He kicked Robin away and picked up the Fear Mask transmitter. It still sputtered sparks.

"This ends now, Dr. Crane!" said Robin.

He kicked the villain hard in the stomach and knocked the wind out of him.

THUMP!

"No," Scarecrow wheezed. "It ends with Batman experiencing every fear all at once!"

Scarecrow furiously punched the transmitter's buttons, desperate for it to do something, anything.

And it did. Atop the train, the remaining gas canisters fired all at once.

Batman was sprayed with the entire complement of fear toxin.

"No!" yelled Robin.

But the Boy Wonder was in full swing, sweeping his staff at Scarecrow's legs from beneath him. The villain crashed to the ground.

THUD!

The back of his head hit the pavement hard, knocking him out.

ON THE TRAIN...

Batman's hands trembled as he unhooked a grapnel gun from his Utility Belt. He did his best to steady his aim.

FOOSH!

He fired the grappling hook into the air. The line spooled out, then tightened. It yanked Batman upward and into the shadows of the nearby buildings.

Nightwing saw Batman soar away. He shouted into his voice transmitter, "Robin! How can I help him?"

Blocks away, Tim thought hard. "You'll have to find a way to make him face his fears and overcome them. There's no other option."

Nightwing sighed. *Easier said than done,* he thought.

FWOOSH!

FWIRSH!

Nightwing leaped from the train and fired his own grapnel into the Gotham City night. He sailed through the air.

As storm clouds rumbled overhead, Nightwing feared that this evening would not end well.

ABOVE THE STREETS...

Batman climbed through the fear. Overhead, past the tops of the buildings, the coming storm announced itself.

CRACKLE!

BOOM!

Batman shivered as the sky boomed and rain began to fall.

"Brontophobia, the fear of thunder," Batman muttered. "Ombrophobia, the fear of rain." He looked down. His stomach turned. "Barophobia, the fear of gravity . . ."

Batman climbed onto a stone gargoyle to steady himself. He was more than twenty stories above the streets now, but at least he had something solid to hold on to.

Suddenly . . .

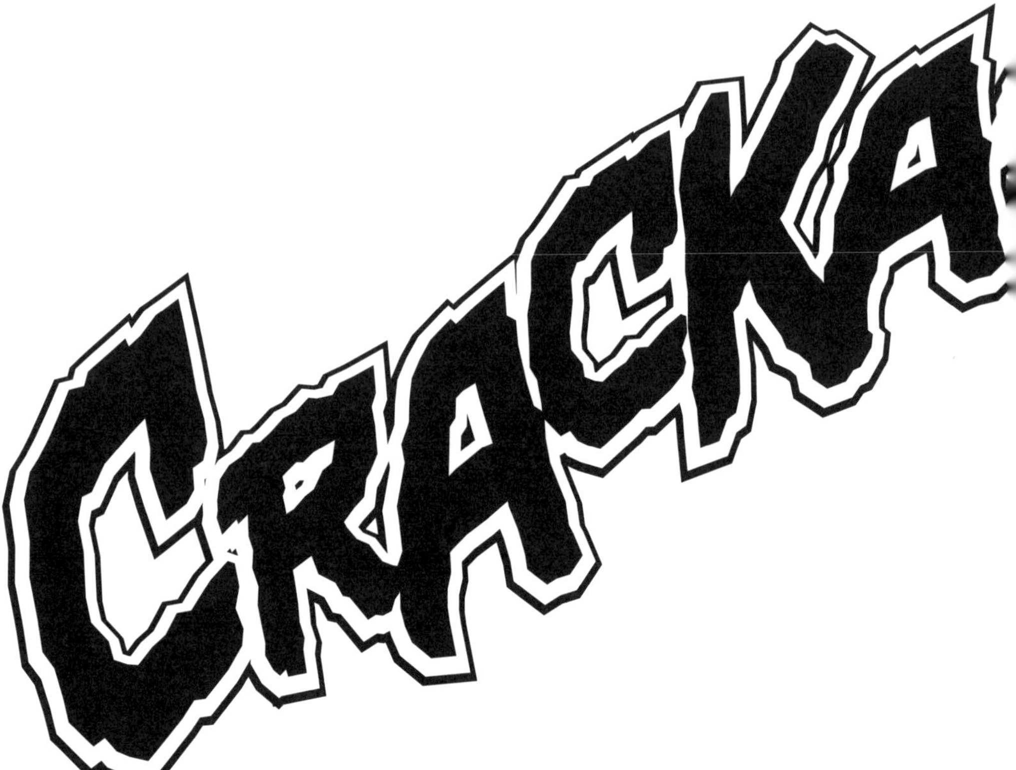
CRACKA

. . . Lightning flashed, and Batman caught sight of the gargoyle's grotesque face. He recoiled in terror.

"Don't worry," someone said from below him. "You're not alone."

Batman looked down the side of the building to see his friend, Nightwing. He tried to smile, but couldn't.

"What are you afraid of?" asked Nightwing.

"Right now?" Batman said. "Falling."

"Then let's conquer that fear," Nightwing said. "Together."

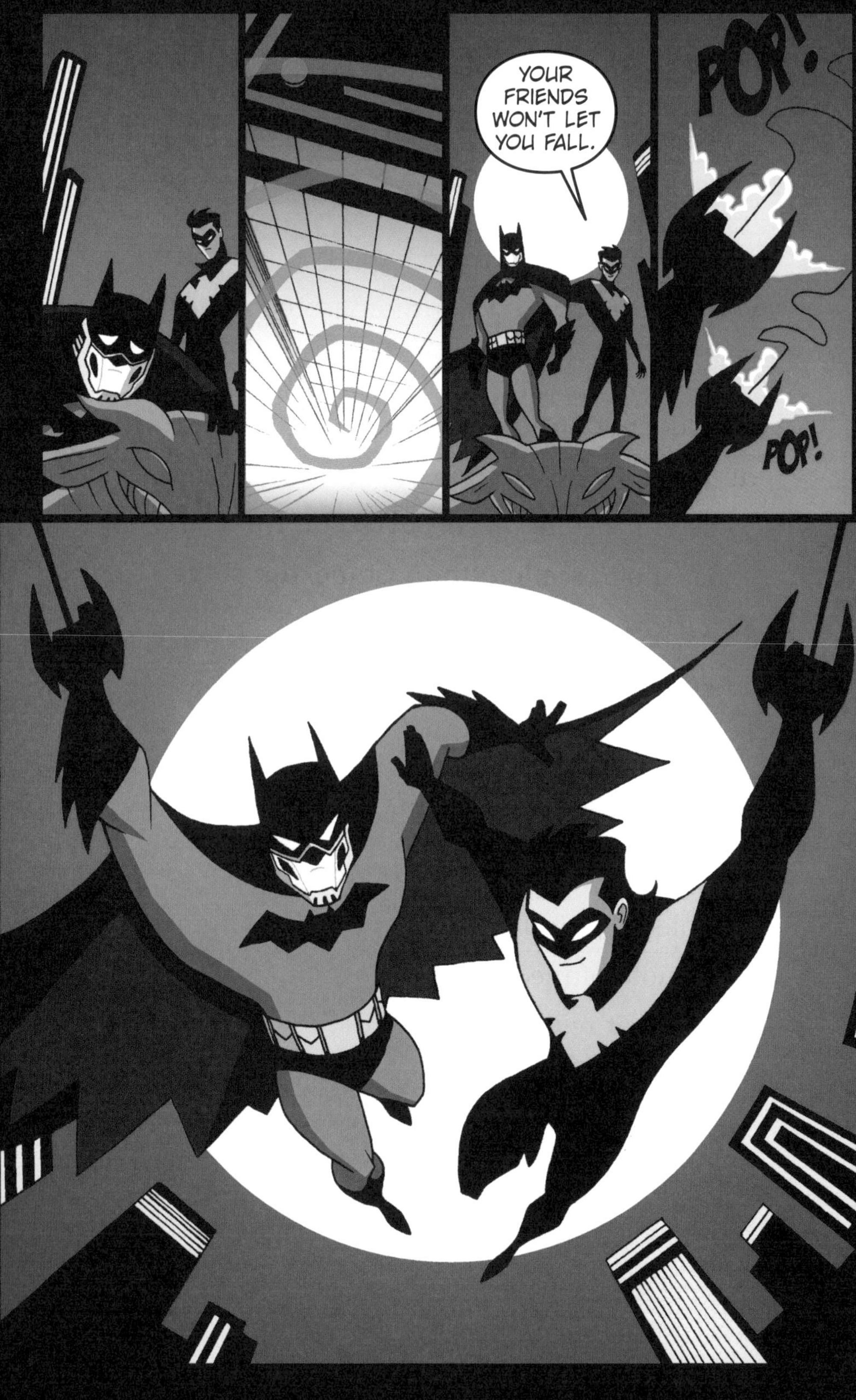
YOUR FRIENDS WON'T LET YOU FALL.
POP!
POP!

Commissioner James Gordon yawned. He was on his way to the early morning roll call at Gotham City Police Department Headquarters.

Suddenly he spied a gangly silhouette seated at the base of a lamppost. Gordon spilled some of his coffee on his overcoat. He wasn't expecting to see Jonathan Crane, a.k.a. the Scarecrow, gift-wrapped for him.

"You startled me, Mr. Crane," said Commissioner Gordon.

"That's what I do," replied the Scarecrow.

The villain's mask was off and he looked completely exhausted. The Boy Wonder had left a note pinned to the Scarecrow's sackcloth costume. It read:

ARREST ME!

"You have the right to remain silent," said Gordon. "And please exercise that right — at least until I've finished my first cup of coffee for the day."

EXITING GOTHAM CITY...

Usually, the Dark Knight and his partners were home well before sunrise. But this morning, Nightwing piloted the Batcycle home while the Batmobile followed close behind.

Robin was at the wheel while Batman slept soundly in the passenger seat.

The Fear Helmet had been safely removed. It resided in the Batmobile's trunk. Tim and Bruce would dismantle it later to learn its secrets — and make sure it didn't fall into the wrong hands ever again.

"Better get back to the Batcave before we're spotted," said Nightwing over the radio.

"Agreed," Robin said.

The Boy Wonder accelerated the Batmobile to catch up.

Batman stirred. "Heliophobia," he muttered softly.

"What's that, Bruce?" asked Nightwing.

Batman sat up in passenger seat. "You're both afraid of sunlight," he said. Then he began to chuckle.

Both Boy Wonders laughed.

BACK AT THE BATCAVE...

Alfred was waiting for the trio of heroes as they parked the vehicles. He greeted them as they approached.

Tim told the faithful servant about the night's adventure.

Nightwing and Robin helped Batman to stand and steadied him as he walked to a waiting stretcher.

And Alfred prepared an antidote for the Scarecrow's fear toxin.

As they passed the giant flat screen display of the Batcomputer, Robin noticed a digital avatar of Alfred. The video game was paused and Alfred was frozen mid-punch as he fought a digital Bane.

Alfred was apparently winning when he'd left the game to cater to his boys.

"You beat the Joker, Alfred?" Tim said, trying — and failing — to conceal his disappointment. "I don't believe it. I haven't gotten past him a single time in the last month."

Alfred nodded as he injected Bruce with the anti-toxin. "It was quite simple, really," he said, straight-faced. "I used a particular fear of mine as motivation."

"And what's that?" Tim asked with more than a fair amount of skepticism.

Alfred shuddered. "A fear of clowns," he said. "They give me the creeps."

Tim and Dick laughed.

Alfred smiled. "There's a tray of sandwiches waiting for you," he said. "I've also warmed the cocoa, young sirs."

The two boys attacked the sandwiches and slurped down the warm drinks with reckless abandon.

"Alfred," Bruce said quietly.

"Yes, Master Bruce?" Alfred asked.

"What are you *really* afraid of?" Bruce asked his trusted butler.

Alfred looked back at Dick and Tim, masks removed, devouring their food. Then he looked back at Bruce.

"I believe it is called eremophobia," said Alfred.

"Fear of being alone?" asked Bruce.

"The fear that you — all of you — might not come home safe," Alfred said.

Alfred covered Bruce with a blanket,

shielding him from the slight chill of the underground Batcave.

"Thankfully, you dispel my fears each and every night," Alfred said.

Bruce smiled.

SCARECROW

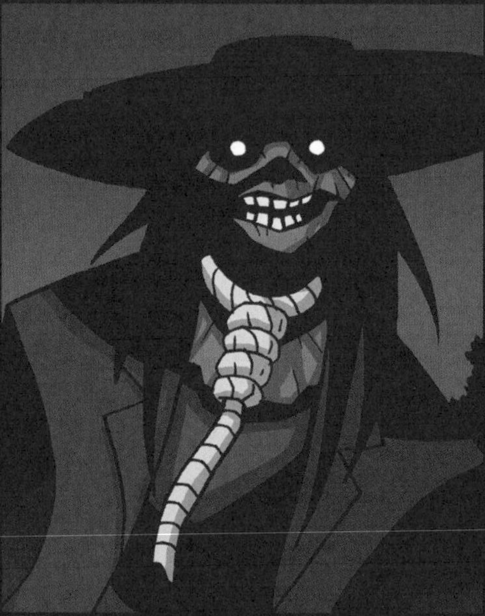

REAL NAME:
Professor Jonathan Crane

OCCUPATION:
Professional Criminal

BASE:
Gotham City

HEIGHT:
6 feet

WEIGHT:
140 pounds

EYES:
Blue

HAIR:
Brown

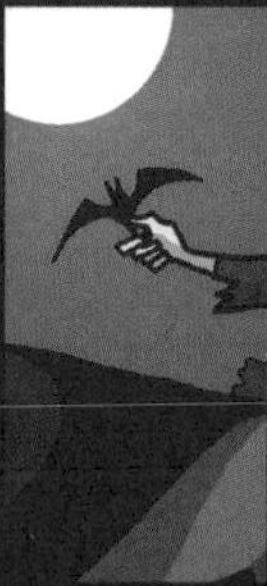

Jonathan Crane's obsession with fear took hold at an early age. Terrorized by bullies, Crane sought to free himself of his own worst fears. As he researched the subject of dread, Crane developed a strong understanding of fear. Using this knowledge, Crane overcame his tormentors by using their worst fears against them. This victory led to his transformation into the creepy super-villain, the Scarecrow.

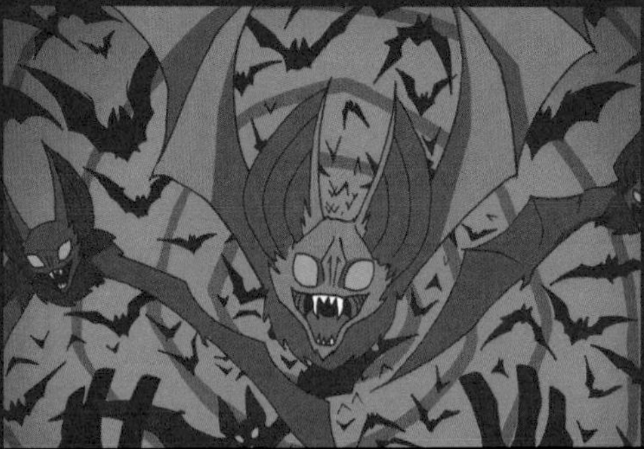

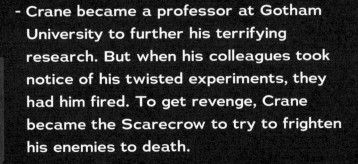

- Crane became a professor at Gotham University to further his terrifying research. But when his colleagues took notice of his twisted experiments, they had him fired. To get revenge, Crane became the Scarecrow to try to frighten his enemies to death.

- Crane doesn't use conventional weaponry. Instead, he invented a fear toxin that causes his victims to hallucinate, bringing their worst fears and phobias to life.

- Even though he preys on the fears of others, the Scarecrow has a fear of his own — bats! Crane has been chiropteraphobic, or afraid of bats, since his first encounter with the Dark Knight.

BIOGRAPHIES

SCOTT BEATTY is the author of many Bat-Books, including The Batman Handbook (Quirk Books), the definitive guide on how to fight crime like the Caped Crusader. He is also the writer of many Bat-Tales for DC Comics, including co-scripting the best-selling Robin Year One, Batgirl Year One, and Nightwing Year One mini-series.

LUCIANO VECCHIO was born in 1982 and currently lives in Buenos Aires, Argentina. With experience in illustration, animation, and comics, his works have been published in the US, Spain, the UK, France, and Argentina. His credits include Ben 10 (DC Comics), Cruel Thing (Norma), Unseen Tribe (Zuda Comics), and Sentinels (Drumfish Productions).

SKETCHES

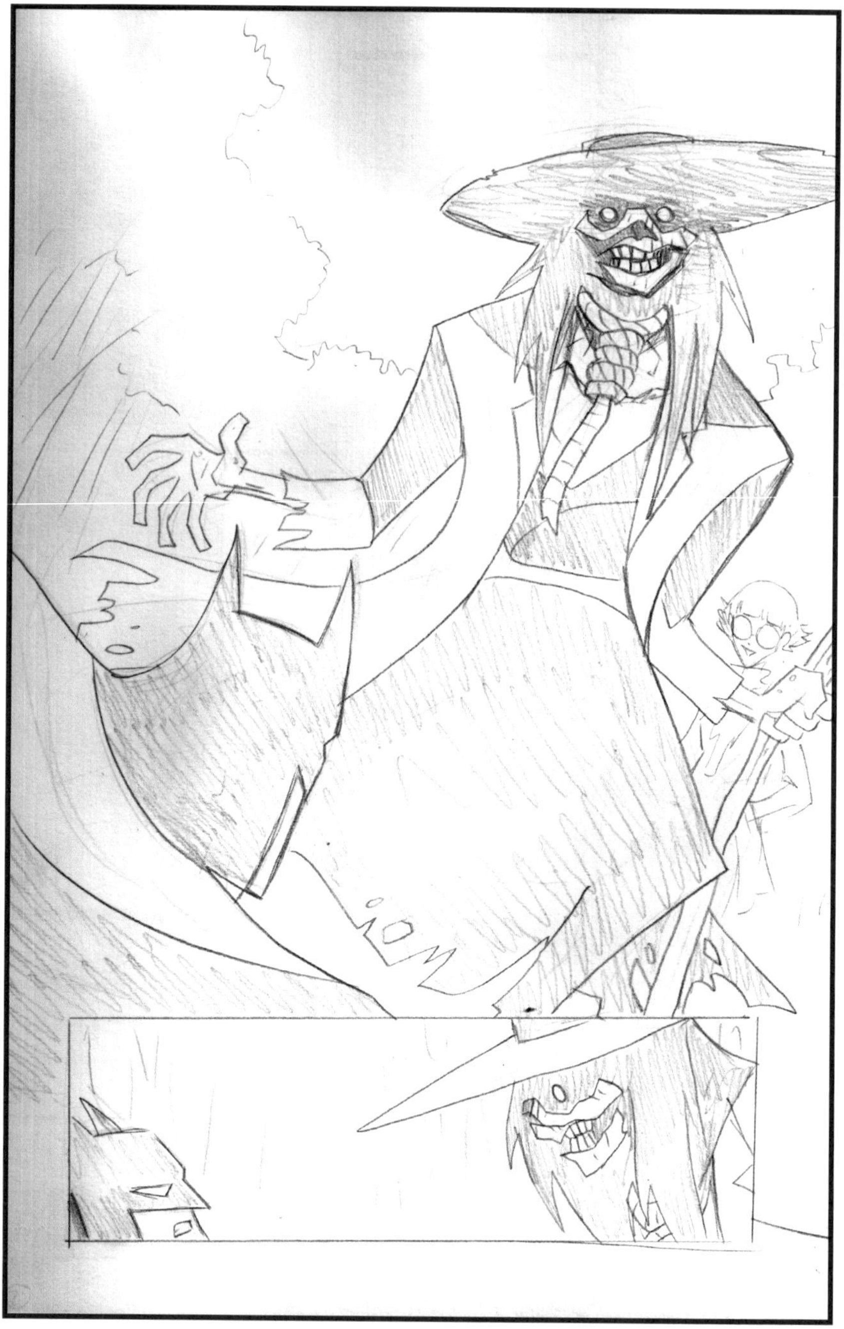

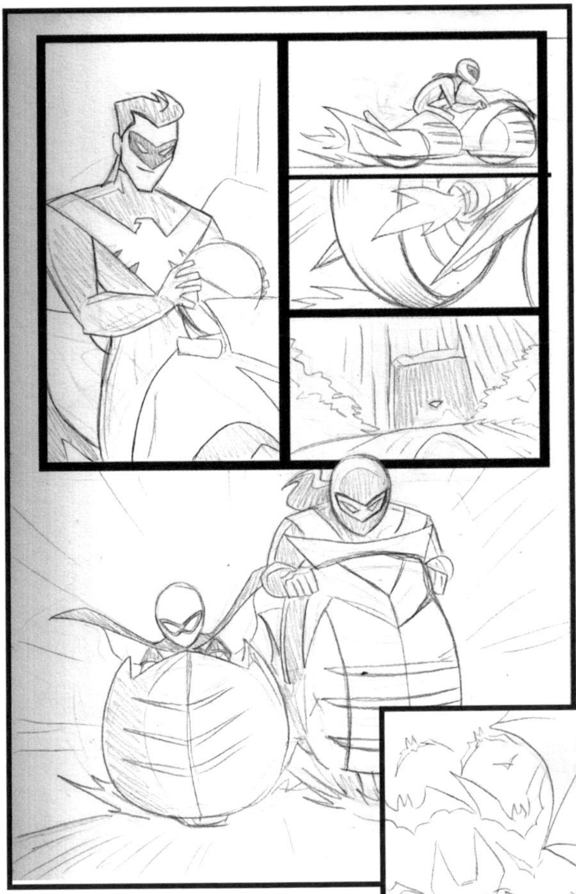

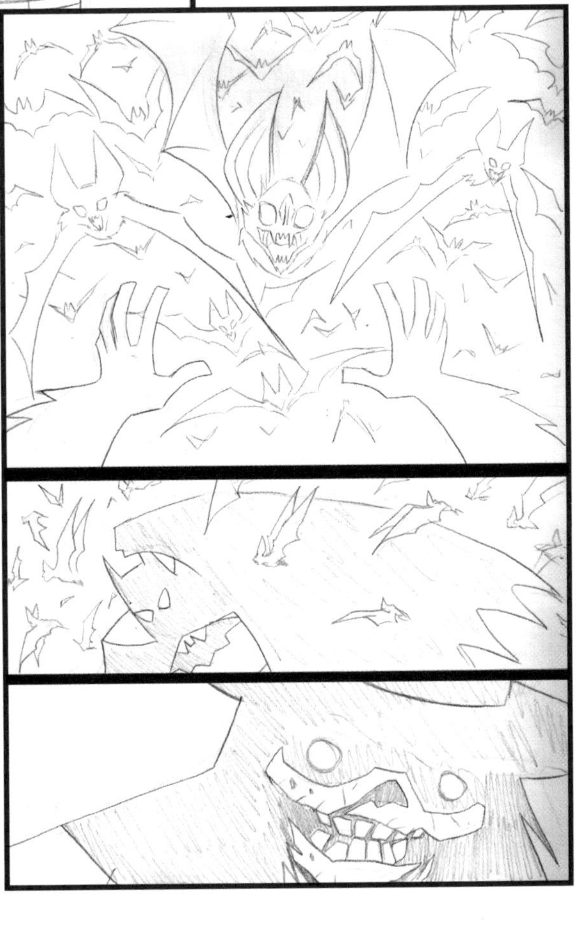

FINAL ART

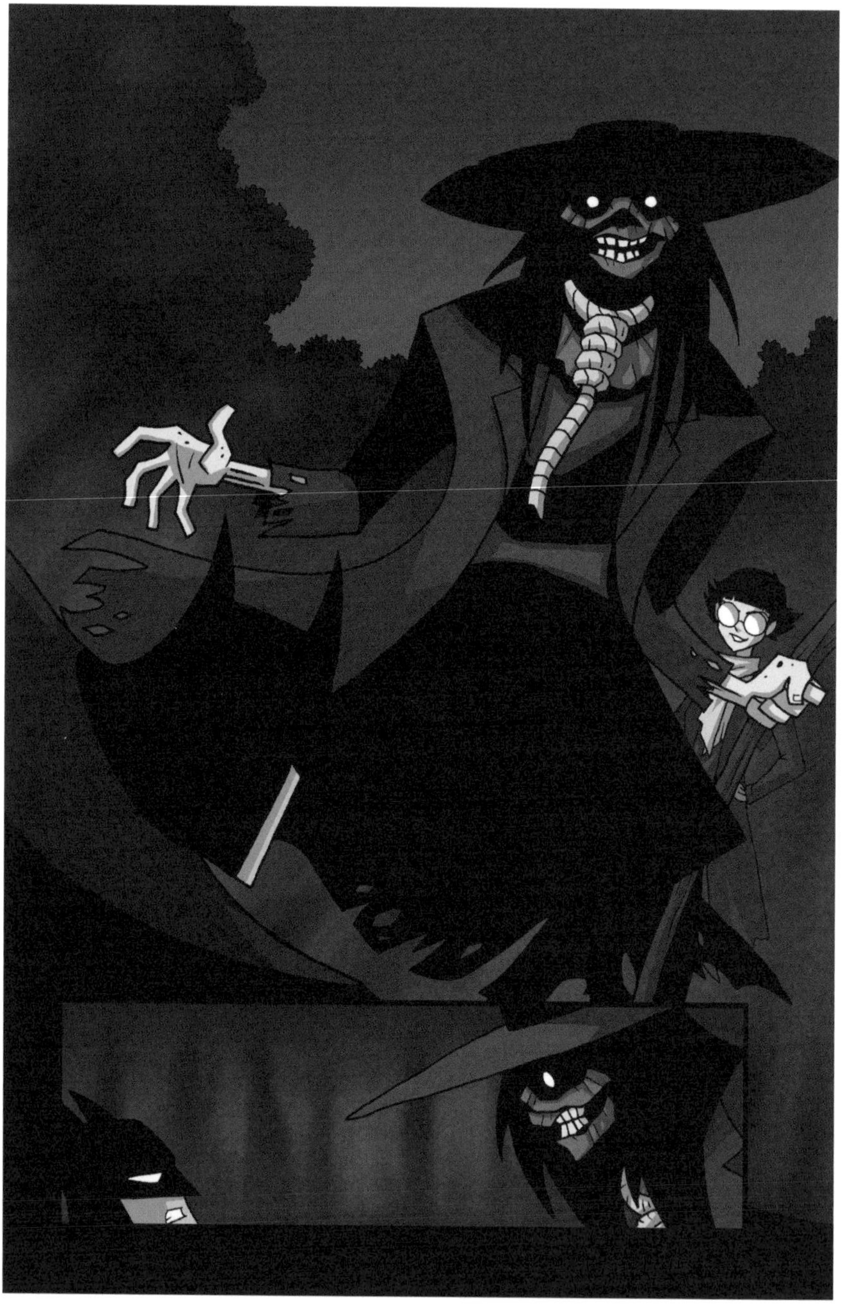

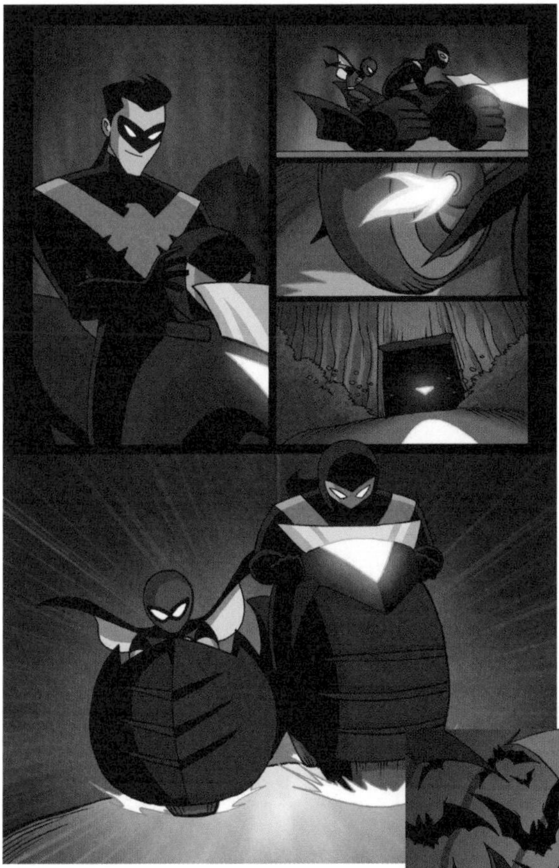
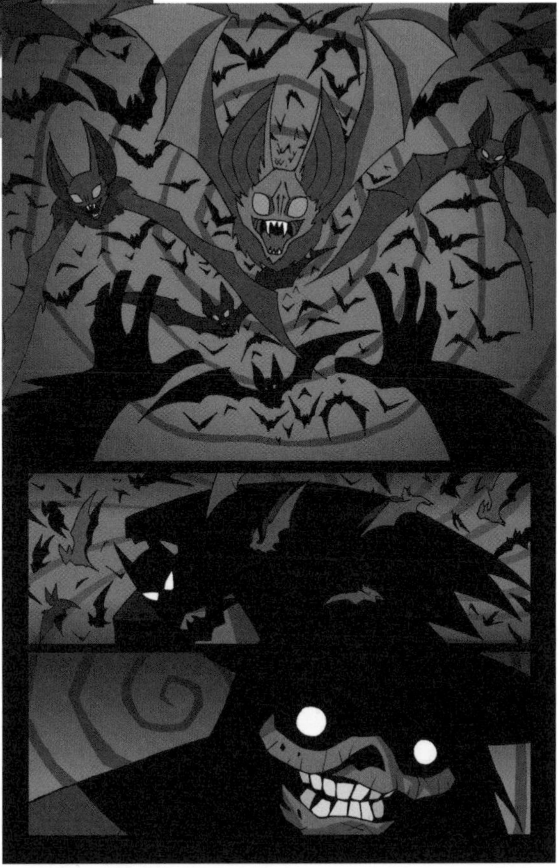

COMICS TERMS

caption (KAP-shuhn)—words that appear in a box. Captions are often used to set the scene.

gutter (GUHT-er)—the space between panels or pages

motion lines (MOH-shuhn LINES)—illustrator-created marks that help show motion in art

panel (PAN-uhl)—a single drawing that has borders around it. Each panel is a separate scene on a spread.

SFX (ESS-EFF-EKS)—short for sound effects. Sound effects are words used to show sounds that occur in the art of a comic.

splash (SPLASH)—a large illustration that often covers a full page (or more)

spread (SPRED)—two side-by-side pages in a comic book

word balloon (WURD BUH-loon)—a speech indicator that includes a character's dialogue or thoughts. A word balloon's tail leads to the speaking character's mouth.

GLOSSARY

abyss (uh-BISS)—a deep, immeasurable space; great nothingness

cowering (KOW-er-ing)—backing away or hunching over due to fear

cowl (KOWL)—the hood of a garment, or the mask and hood of a super hero

disintegrated (diss-IN-tuh-grayt-id)—broke apart into many smalls pieces

elongated (i-LONG-gayt-id)—if something is elongated, it is longer than normal

incapacitated (in-kuh-PASS-i-tay-tid)—made unable to work, move, or function

labyrinth (LAB-uh-rinth)—a place with many confusing twists and turns

patrol (pah-TROHL)—the act of walking around an area in order to make sure that it's safe

thwarted (THWAR-tid)—prevented something from happening or ruined someone's plans

toxin (TAWK-sin)—a poisonous substance

VISUAL QUESTIONS

1. What did Batman do on page 18 in these two panels? Why didn't he want his mask removed?

2. Why does Scarecrow look this way on page 19's final panel? Whose perspective are we seeing from?

3. Are the images with the arrows and animals signs or panels? Read the definition of "panel" on the previous page. What is the difference between a sign and a panel?

4. What did Nightwing do to help Batman in these three panels? What other ways did Robin and Nightwing help Batman in this book?

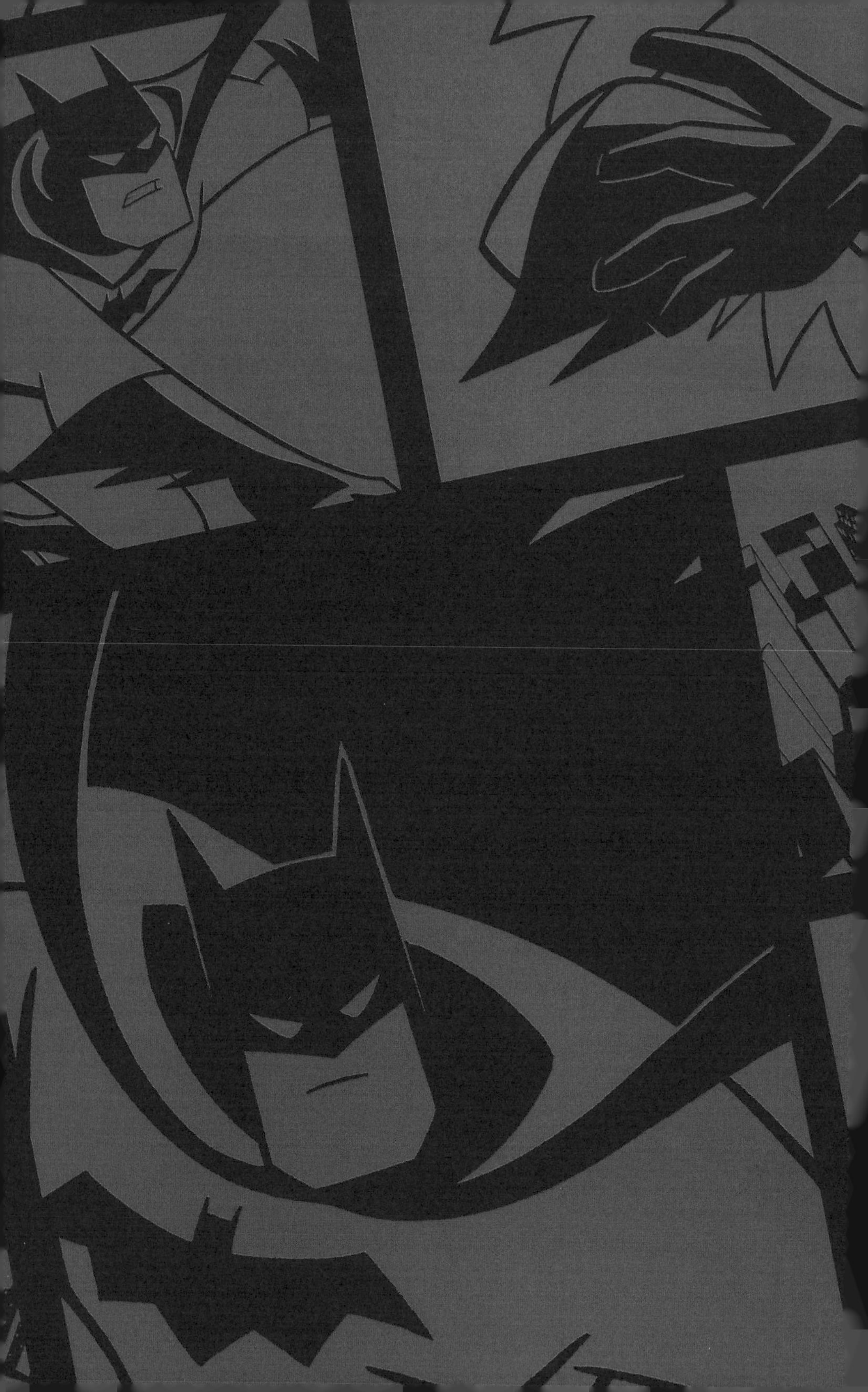

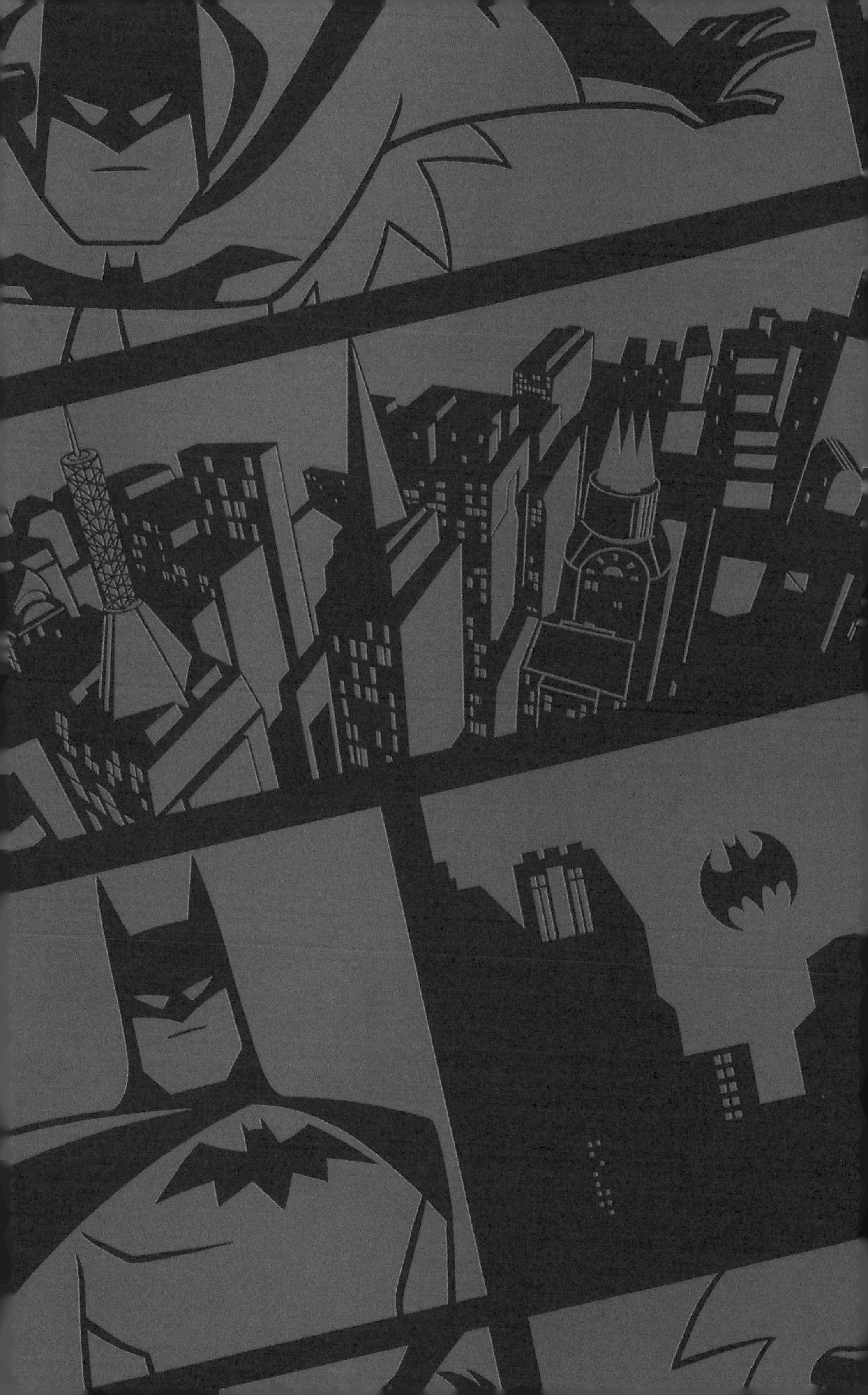